Mel Bay's Book of
the Dead

Mel Bay's Book of the Dead

stories

Harold Whit Williams

SAR Press
Austin

Library of Congress Cataloging-in-Publication Data
Names: Williams, Harold Whit. | Williams, Harold Whit, 10/11/
1968–. Mel Bay's Book of the Dead.
Title: Mel Bay's Book of the Dead
Description: Trade paperback edition. | Austin: SAR Press/William
O. Pate II, 2021.
Identifiers: LCCN 2021900688| ISBN 9781736177921 (softcover)

Published by
SAR Press/William O. Pate II
an imprint of *San Antonio Review*
2028 E. Ben White Boulevard #240-5735
Austin, Texas 78741
United States of America

"Touchdown, Alabama" originally published on October 25, 2020, in
San Antonio Review (Volume IV, Fall 2020).
Available online at DOI: 10.21428/9b43cd98.afdd3e3e

Cover art by Ashley Savage Williams.

The first collection of short stories published by SAR Press, Austin,
Texas, USA.

The publisher's father, William O. Pate, has converted former family
farmland in southwest Alabama into new growth forest and enrolled
it in the U.S. Department of Agriculture's Conservation Reserve
Program in support of climate-change mitigation, covering at least a
portion of the renewable resources required to produce print
editions of this book.

Always read free at sareview.org

This page intentionally left blank for prisoners without access to paper.

From the midst of that radiance, the natural sound of Reality, reverberating like a thousand thunders simultaneously sounding, will come. That is the natural sound of thine own real self. Be not daunted thereby, nor terrified, nor awed.

— *Tibetan Book of the Dead*

The time I burned my guitar it was like a sacrifice.

You sacrifice the things you love.

— *Jimi Hendrix*

Contents

Touchdown, Alabama   1

Firebreathing for Beginners   4

Fighting Joe Wheeler   12

Japanese Fanclub   21

Destination Dollywood   33

Preacher Down   37

Why Standest Thou Afar, O Lord?   45

The Happy Hitters Sing Songs of Praise   59

The Second Hurricane   66

Me and the Devil Blues   79

Dwayne from Texas   88

The Body is a Temple   101

Pine Grove Blues   104

Mel Bay's Book of the Dead   116

Acknowledgements   129

About the Author   130

Other Works by Harold Whit Williams   131

About the Publisher   132

Touchdown, Alabama

A late September Saturday afternoon. The sky godless and electric blue and filled with trumpet blast and statistics. What a tiny scab on this roadmap Touchdown is, but would you look at that stadium! Worthy of the vilest gladiator games. And, now, a crowd of townsfolk appears, a sweaty biological mass of many moving as one, willing itself towards relevancy. They scuttle past in a harsh slanted light. Their mouths snap open and shut like sea turtles.

They say — Go State.

Snap.

They say — Beat Tech.

Snap.

They say — We're number one and so on and so forth.

Snap snap snap.

The town, having been founded by some fur trapper of dubious French legend way back in the buck-skinned year of eighteen and *blah blah bla— did you see that monster truck yonder?!* Covered in State stickers and flags. Horn blaring the State fight song. Go State! Muffler blast of yon truck. Beat Tech! *Rat-a-tat* of marching band snare and tom. Hot white flash of damp cheerleader panties. Sacrificial teenaged flesh, sweaty and bare. Old men devouring their young with gauzy-going eyes.

And look! Right there in the shady square beneath granite Jeb Stuart upon his horse — it is the town derelict, standing atop a park bench and shouting.

"Idolaters! Heretics!"

He makes a bullhorn of his filthy hands and shouts, "Hypocrites on parade! Love thy enemy!"

His beard a tangled owl's nest, his face the texture and color of oak bark. Townsfolk shuffle past, oblivious. Glances here and there. Gravel and hard candy cast upon him by trailer trash children, then snickering.

"Oh, the poor shall always be among us! Poor in health. Poor of mind. Poor in the Holy Spirit!" the derelict continues.

The derelict's name is Gaylord Gunn Godd, Ph.D. Long ago, this man, a much-lauded thinker and writer, with an East Coast doctorate in Ancient Rhetoric or Meta-Religious Studies or Philosophical Poetics or some such horseshit. Upon retirement, he gave up office hours and tramped abroad for several years (war-torn Latin America, drab Eastern Europe) only to find himself returning to Touchdown and squatting in the back room of a meth lab ranch-style two miles out on the highway. Doctor Godd, the hick tenants call him. He hath blessed us, they say between pipe sucks. Fits of sick laughter and wet coughing. Godd be with us, *har har*.

Sky a softer blue now, with high wispy cirrus in the north. The marching band townsfolk parade has moved on down Champion Street and now fills the stadium with such Old Testament noise. Sun dropping behind tall pines. Far-off hum of the highway. Nighthawks zigzagging above.

There is no one left in the square but Doctor Godd. He still stands atop the bench, stroking his tangled beard, huffing and puffing. The air suddenly reeks of papermill, of popcorn, of sad-eyed surrender. He turns slowly around to face the stadium and shouts.

"Blessed are the meek for they shall inherit the earth!"

He shouts, "Faith without works is dead!"

He shouts, "Beware of false prophets!"

A rumbling now from down the street, overtaking the game noise. His bench is quaking, but Gaylord stays put, still staring at the stadium. Like riding a surfboard, he is, laughing and pointing now as the giant lights flicker and go out. He can just catch a multitude of screams on the wind. A weeping and gnashing of teeth. Again, he shouts.

"And the rain descended, and the floods came, and the winds blew, and beat upon that house; and it fell: and great was the fall of it!"

A pause. A nighthawk *keers* overhead. Then, a prehistoric boom, and the stadium collapses in on itself like in some motion picture nightmare. Champion Street crumbles into a gaping maw. A crevasse to hell. Doctor Godd screams his laughter now. Screams to the silent heavens. He places his filthy hands together in prayer, and then drops like a stone with the rest of Touchdown into the black and unforgiving earth.

Firebreathing for
Beginners

I come from a long line of unobservant men. Mr. Magoo-types plodding about the planet and squinting at everything through bespectacled eyes. Men who quietly hold down their low-paying small-town day jobs. Men who live off sandwiches and beer and watch TV and go to bed early and call up other men handier than themselves to take care of things around the house more complicated than mowing the lawn or sweeping the carport. Which is how you come to find me now, sitting here inebriated in this stifling hot Mexican cantina.

I doubt you'll ask — men like myself rarely get asked questions. So, I'll tell you anyway.

My name is Sebastian. My girlfriend of seven years, Norma, left me recently for a firefighter she met in Dallas. I'm slightly effeminate and teach guitar lessons out at the community center off Highway 79. Folk-rock is my forte, but I've been known to hit a power chord now and then. My town has quite a few fellows like myself (lightly-bearded, readers of poetry, et cetera) but legions more are knuckle-draggers, meth-heads, hillbilly plant workers — wild-eyed and aggressive alpha chimps always on the lookout for something or someone to physically assault or dry hump or both.

The average IQ around here is shockingly low. Most likely from the nearby chemical plant or pesticide runoff. And, concerning those alpha chimps seeking their prey, I eat dinner early with the elderly in a hospital cafeteria and stay off the streets when darkness falls.

Oh, yes — why you've come to find me here: my plumber friend, Walter, is an avid birdwatcher. This surprised me to hear, I must say. He was fixing my stopped-up toilet one Saturday afternoon and somehow the conversation came around to his pet parrot, Peter. Peter is a green parrot native to Mexico. I recall staring down in amazement at Walter's ass crack while listening to him rattle off all the different species and subspecies of parrots, parakeets, macaws and cockatoos. He and his wife had an upcoming trip planned to photograph the flora and fauna of some cloud forest preserve west of Tampico. However, because of her work schedule, she would now not be able to go.

"Why don't you come along?" Walter asked. He undoubtedly felt sorry for me, what with my ghosting about in this mostly empty three-bedroom bungalow. "I see those finch feeders in your backyard." I do, in fact, have finch feeders, and have long kept a list of species sighted upon my little plot of city land. "You just wouldn't believe the variety of birds down there," he continued. "Just south of the Tropic of Cancer, the overall species count goes way up. It's amazing." His face beamed like just-cleaned porcelain.

So, I canceled a few lessons and took Walter up on his proposition. We pulled out of my driveway in a sad March rain. For just a second, I swore I saw Norma peeking out through the front window curtains, but then I blinked and remembered that she's gone. Walter steered us south in his Ford F-150, pointing out roadside hawks, black vultures, and caracaras. We made good time and crossed the border at Brownsville only to crawl through the tiny crowded streets of Matamoros. As we were sitting and waiting at the umpteenth traffic light, Walter picked that very moment to mention the recent cartel violence down here. The Gulf hombres versus the Zetas. Tortures. Beheadings. Mass executions of bus riders. He talked about how bad it's gotten of late and said that the tour guides where we're going might cancel these trips soon. I wondered why he waited to tell me all of this until we were sitting like proverbial ducks at a redlight in the narco-state of Tamaulipas, but then I remembered that I'm a Mr. Magoo-type. Unobservant and all that. Maybe he did mention this as he was unplugging the stopped-up shit in my toilet while I was staring down at his ass crack. Or maybe he didn't.

We were booked at the fancy gringo hotel in Ciudad Mante. Mante is a dry and dusty ranchero city sitting at the base of the Sierra Madre Oriental near the San Luis Potosi state line. Walter speaks fluent Spanish, and even more importantly, he tells me, fluent Mexican. He knows all the swear words and can yell and puff out his chest like some machismo El Jefe.

We tossed our bags into the oven-hot room and headed downstairs to the bar. Walter wanted to get me acclimated to the whole mañana vibe. He said a shot or two is in order. And so here we sit, dear reader. By dinnertime, I've lost count of the tequilas consumed and suddenly I can't recognize those two faces in the long mirror behind the bartender. They are greasy and sunburnt, and they keep laughing at all those stupid jokes we're telling.

The next morning finds us blurry-eyed and nauseous in the hillside village of Gomez Farias. Melodious blackbirds are making a racket in the strangler fig and mango thicket above us. Juan, our tour guide, keeps glancing at his wristwatch and scanning the gravel road that will lead us up into the mountains. He seems a tad nervous to me, but Walter lumbers about without a care in the world. Prime parrot viewing in the canopies up there, he had boasted last night at the bar. At least, that's what I think he said.

Juan's army Jeep bumps us up and over the twisting steep grades and higher and higher into the Sierra. We stop every so often for Walter to photograph rare cloud forest flowers or green jays or to take a leak.

"Take care," Juan says in his fine English. "Fer-de-lance in tall grass." Walter turns his head back from pissing and expounds.

"Watch for vipers off the trail. A birder last year got bit and carted back to Texas in a pine box."

After a simple bean and nopales and tortilla lunch, the afternoon drags on. No siesta for us on this birdwatching death march. It is unbelievably hot. Tropic of Cancer hot. Juan and Walter confab in Spanish at every stop and Walter seems to gain energy and strength as each hour passes. I always had this idea that I was some sort of naturalist. Some sort of low-rent amateur ornithologist. Turns out, I'm just another hobbyist schmuck who falls asleep drunk on the couch watching *Animal Planet*. Juan whistles sharply and points upwards into a blooming jacaranda tree. A blue-crowned motmot is showily perched in the highest bough, perfectly posed for Walter's camera. "Holy shit," he whispers between all the snapping. "Holy shit."

Later that afternoon at the hotel bar, we pace ourselves, and, between Tecate sips, Walter giggles and rattles off new additions to his life list. Mountain trogon, blue mockingbird, military macaw. I could go on, of course, but will not. Truthfully, the spectacular avifauna of this trip has become dull and dreary for me in less than twenty-four hours. I realize just how much I miss Norma. The vile, selfish bitch. Giving up on me, on us, after the better part of a decade invested. Giving it all up for some young hardbody pumping his daily chin-ups and saving lives and property up in the metroplex area. Asshole. Assholes, one and all. "Mas tequila, por favor!" I shout out to nobody.

It is then that I spy the young waitress slicing limes. Her coffee complexion and her jet-black pixie cut. Her breasts high and pressed tight in a fitted white dress shirt. I imagine the dark nipples underneath and my mouth roving over them. My tongue rolling perfect Spanish r's, making her laugh and run her fingers lazily through my Dan Fogelberg hair. She would then groan and gently push my head further down. Her casita bedroom window thrown open. Blue sky. Adobe walls. Bougainvillea blossoms bursting into a flaming red outside.

A telephone rings and I look over to find Walter in animated conversation with the bartender, a tiny elderly fellow gesturing with a formal, colonial flair. I swallow the last of my beer, pat Walter on his shoulder, and excuse myself from their company.

With the sun having dropped behind those Sierras to

the west, the zocalo in Mante is awash in a golden hour light. Friday evening, lively and noisy. Bustle of taco truck vendors. Smells of charcoal and grilled meats. Thumping Tejano music in the square. Howling mongrels, crying children. Chopped and welded old Toyotas and VWs blasting past without mufflers. The faintest waft of weed.

I sit on a park bench munching an empanada as grackles squawk and beep in the fan palms above me. At a busy intersection across the square, I see a fellow at the corner spewing flames above the stopped traffic. I hear faint clapping and laughing and notice a couple of people handing him money. The light changes, the cars move on, and the fellow returns to his folding chair and slowly sits down.

It is Juan, our guide from this morning. He looks at me sheepishly as I approach, then winks and gives a thumbs-up like he's seen on gringo TV. He looks exhausted. His lips are glossy from swigging something flammable and his left hand grips a wad of dirty cash notes. In his right hand, a small torch burns. "Juan," I say, "This is incredible. All of this."

He winks at me again and says, "Nice. Nice."

"Can I buy you a cold cerveza, amigo?'

"Nice. Nice."

I return shortly with two tall cans of lukewarm Modelo. He grabs one, smiling, and says, "Nice." His torch is wedged in the arm of his folding chair. A gallon jug sitting beneath. Cars swerve by, some honking, as Juan's flickering flame is tilted out just so into the street. He takes a small sip of beer, spits, then follows with long gulping swigs while eyeing the traffic. He grins and motions for the honking cars to go on by. Then, the light goes red.

Juan crushes his empty and tosses it to the curb. He

grabs his torch and his jug of petrol or whatever it is. Car windows roll down with children's beaming faces poking out. Juan transforms into a street-corner dragon, blowing blue-orange flames up and out into the night sky. Shrieks and applause from the backseat children. More wadded-up bills. The light goes green.

I am spellbound. I have no idea how much time has passed. After several more rounds of Modelo, I ask Juan why he does this. He looks uncomfortable for a moment, and then his face softens.

"Mi papi fire breathe. His papi fire breathe." The traffic is a bit lighter now, and he waves off a couple of cars waiting at the red-light. "Either this I do, along with tours," he says, "or I sell mota."

I hand Juan the two crumpled hundred-dollar bills I forgot to exchange at the border and stumble off in the general direction of our gringo hotel. My feet ache. My bladder is near bursting. My head is swimming with fermented agave juice and pre-Columbian pagan fire.

Stepping out of the hotel lobby bathroom, I see the elderly bartender closing up for the night. That supple young waitress nowhere to be seen. Walter most likely snoring in our room. My breath comes short and quick. My spleen is throbbing. I pour myself into a plush parlor chair and dial up Norma on my cell phone.

"What?" she croaks.

"I am going to breathe fire, Norma."

"Sebastian?"

"I am going to breathe fire on the street corner, and people will give me money."

Silence on the line. Then, a loud sigh.

"Where are you, Sebastian?"

The elderly fellow is locking up the bar. He glances my way, nods, and plods toward the lobby exit.

"I am going to breathe fire on the street corner, Norma. People will applaud and give me money."

"Damnit Sebastian, what's going on? What are you . . ?"

"I release you, Norma. I release you to your young hardbody lover. I release you to your satellite-dish suburban hellscape Dallas. I release you to bloat and die and rot and to never have mattered a good goddamn to anyone."

I toss my phone down into the mulch of a giant potted ficus, then stoop and pick up Juan's jug of flammable liquid and his unlit torch. I stroll back out through the lobby exit, the doorman not even batting an eye.

Fighting Joe Wheeler

Every morning since seventh grade started, Mama drops me off at the curb up the street from school. Our car is a Pontiac with much rust the color of dog shit. My only friend, TJ, has seen it and even ridden in it and doesn't care, but I don't want anyone else to know that this is our car. When Daddy picks me up on weekends, he points at it and says,

Joe, you know what Pontiac means?

No, I always say, grinning.

He says,

It's a Cherokee word meaning *fill me up again.*

Then Daddy always laughs and coughs. His belly is round and catfish pale and shows a hairy bit when his T-shirt rides up. He lights a Camel and says

Pam, why you still driving this thing?

He says,

Pam, this car is the color of a two-toned BM.

He says,

Pam, I swear I saw this thing floating in the breakroom commode back at Wal-Mart. Damn thing just wouldn't flush.

More laughing and coughing as Mama frowns and

shakes her head and goes back inside and slams the door without saying goodbye. She frowns and slams the door a lot of late. And, just the other day, I caught her crying at a stoplight. I asked her what was wrong, but she said not to worry. Just grown-up stuff. But, Mama does drop me off at the curb away from school. This is maybe the only thing nice she does for me — other than food and shelter and laundry and helping me with geometry.

Daddy sleeps late on Saturdays. It's his day off from stocking the warehouse and he's taken pills for his back and had a lot of Friday night beers, as he calls them. So, he stays in bed until noon or later. We sometimes toss the football or just sit around and watch cartoons or a game or something. But mostly he's out on the back porch smoking and drinking beer. He keeps saying that he'll take the both of us up to that state park with the lake so we can watch the geese, but we haven't gone yet. The park is named for a Civil War general, Fighting Joe Wheeler. I read that he was at Shiloh, at the Bloody Pond, and that he killed a bunch of Indians out West. My name is also Joe Wheeler, son of Billy and Pam Wheeler, but Mama says we're not related to the general and that they named me Joseph from the Bible instead.

So, Daddy's asleep, and I'm eating a bowl of Count Chocula and listening to the radio. It's only eight-thirty but TJ is already in our front yard doing circles on his Huffy. He keeps popping wheelies and yelling out *Yay-eee* like that Cajun chef on TV. I step outside and tell him to be quiet because Daddy is sleeping. TJ stops his bike and stares back at me. He has snot running out both nostrils because it's the first cold morning in October. A shower of red leaves falls behind him and his eyes look dark and mean.

Your daddy's just a drunk, he shouts.

He spins his bike around and pedals off down the driveway and into the street.

Mama told me once that TJ has a wild streak in him because he's Greek. Greek or Slavic or Gypsy. She says that after the long boat ride over here, his family name was changed from Mikos or Milosevic or something like that to Michaels to sound more American. (TJ stands for Thomas Jefferson, he always says.) But their Sunday afternoon get-togethers are loud and lively and filled with much food and wine and laughter and song and don't seem very American to me, regardless of their new name. Our family get-togethers only happen around Easter or Christmas, and they are usually quiet and seem kind of sad. On occasion, Grandmother might holler out for Jesus when Daddy says grace. He'll sneak a peek over at me when she does that, and we both have to try hard to not start giggling. But TJ's family get-togethers remind me of something I read about in a *National Geographic*. Some story about the customs and traditions observed on a dry and windy Turkish island. All the men drinking and dancing. The women slaughtering goats and swatting flies. Another thing, TJ tans darkly while I simply turn pink and blister and fade. Do all of these things explain his "wild streak," as Mama says? I think not. But maybe?

TJ is a strange one. He cuts classes and bikes all over town singing *put the lime in the coconut* and *ride captain ride upon your mystery ship*. He climbs those spindly mimosa trees out beside the highway and hoots at passing traffic like a howler monkey. He told me once that his granddaddy, a sheepherder back in the old country, would take young girls up into a secret cave in the mountains and molest them. He said all this matter-of-factly, in the same way I would tell someone my granddaddy sang in a gospel quartet or served on city council.

At first period history class on Monday, Miss Howell announces a field trip for the week before Halloween. Turns out we're going up to Joe Wheeler State Park. She points at it on our big map of Alabama and asks us to please bring our signed permission slips back by the end of the week. I can't believe my luck, and can hardly wait to hop into that dog-shit Pontiac and tell Mama where we're going.

That sounds fun, Mama says, fussing with her bangs in the rearview mirror. We've barely pulled away from the curb when she starts talking about her day at work. She's a secretary at the dentist's office and she always whines about rude patients. Bitch and moan, she says, bitch and moan. Which is funny because I realize that's exactly what she does around me. Suddenly, I'm not that excited about my school trip anymore. I notice that all the old houses and trailers blurring past us on the highway look empty and abandoned. I bet they're cold inside. I bet if folks still live in them, they are lonely and sad and drift from room to room like ghosts no one can see.

Daddy asks,
Where's TJ at?
I'm flipping through the latest issue of my *Sergeant Rock* comic book and half-watching a PBS show about cheetahs. I've already read that they are the fastest land animals on Earth. Falcons are faster, but they fall through

the sky and get help from their wings and all. The new comic book has a nice inky smell. I breathe it in deep and say that TJ is camping with his big brothers out in Sipsey Wilderness. I have no idea what TJ is doing really, as he hasn't talked to me since I asked him to be quiet out in Daddy's yard. I lie because I'm embarrassed to think that my friend doesn't like me anymore. But now I have this signed permission slip for our class trip, and I get excited again about visiting the park and seeing all those geese. I'm so excited that I forget about TJ on his Huffy doing circles in our yard and how dark and mean his eyes looked.

A few years back, TJ and I were playing Chickasaw Indians with our toy bow and arrows at the edge of a sage-grass pasture behind his house. We stopped to gorge ourselves upon ripe blackberries growing in a wild bramble along a fence. The purple-red juice soon stained our fingers and lips, and we laughed about how one might mistake it for blood. A strange look came over TJ's face, and he reached down into the pocket of his blue jeans and pulled out a small switchblade.

We should become blood brothers, he whispered.

His face contained a graven look, as if he was sitting up front row in church on a Sunday morning. Thunder rumbled in the distance. A crow cawed from the other side of the pasture. I held out my left hand, palm up, and took a deep breath.

Our class is filing onto the idling school bus for the trip to Wheeler. It's early Monday morning, still dark and cold. I walk down the aisle past TJ, who is sitting with a boy whose name I cannot recall. TJ and the boy are laughing and pointing out the window at something in the parking lot, and I'm suddenly afraid that Mama forgot to give me something for the trip and had to pull up in her dog-shit Pontiac beside the bus to come aboard and give it to me. I glance outside and spy Miss Howell at her Ford Pinto. She's bent over digging something out of her trunk. Her big fat ass is stuck up in the air and wiggling about, so I'm relieved to see that it's not my mama and our car.

There's an empty seat on the back row for me and my binoculars and my peanut butter sandwich sack lunch. I sit down beside Dawn, a red-haired girl I sort of know from history class.

Hey, she says, smiling a toothy grin filled with braces.

She says,

I was just saving this seat for you.

She says,

We don't have school today, Joe, isn't that great?

She lightly touches my left arm and giggles and says we're going to *your* park!

I smile and giggle and cannot help but think of Daddy in his bed still asleep. I always pictured him taking me to Wheeler, and now I'm going without him. It feels strange, but also kind of thrilling. Maybe, one day, I'll be a bus driver and travel to all the different state parks.

Dawn stays beside me the whole morning at the park. She even holds my hand on the little boardwalk trail over the marsh and out to the lake's edge. There's still a chill in the air but Dawn's hand is hot and scaly. There are strips of fog hanging onto the tops of the trees, but as we approach the lookout pier it clears up and we can see hundreds of geese floating and flapping out upon the water's surface. I share my binoculars with Dawn.

She says,

Oh, wow, when a whole bunch of geese lift off at once

and skim the lake coming towards us. They pull up at the last second and veer off above our heads and above the tops of the trees behind us. Oh wow, she says again.

We tour the Wheeler home, which is filled with furniture and paintings and boring stuff that none of my classmates care about. Later, out on the plantation grounds, Miss Howell sets up picnic blankets for our sack lunches. The day has cleared and become Indian summer warm. I look around and find TJ and that other boy standing off to the edge of the clearing. Neither of them have lunches. They're still laughing at something, maybe the same thing from earlier this morning, and they're hooting and hollering and ripping bark off a pine tree and throwing pinecones hard at each other. Miss Howell shouts at them to sit down and behave. Dawn and I share a blanket with a couple of her friends, but she wiggles over next to me with her lunch. I feel suddenly flushed and a bit nervous with her friends giggling and looking over at the two of us. My stomach has butterflies and I'm not that hungry anymore, so I give Dawn half of my peanut butter sandwich, which she takes and quickly eats, laughing all the while along with her friends.

As we pack up our lunch scraps, Miss Howell goes off with the tour guide into the park headquarters, leaving us all alone with the bus driver. He is leaning up against the back of the bus, smoking a cigarette and flipping through a magazine. I'm just about to tell Dawn about my daddy and how he always meant to bring me here but never did, when I hear a strange yet familiar sound coming from across the grounds. It's TJ yelling out *Yay-ee! Yay-ee!* He's honking like a goose now and sprinting towards me. He honks and screams — this ain't your park! Your daddy is a drunk! Your daddy is a drunk!

The force of his hit puts the both of us down onto the cool grass. The wind is knocked out of me and I gulp for air with loud, pitiful, animal groans. I'm embarrassed for the sounds I'm making, and I can feel all the classroom eyes upon us, especially Dawn's. She has stepped away, I can sense somehow. I am certain that she is red-faced and too ashamed to help. TJ is on top, pounding his fists into my face and chest. In a flash, he opens up his switchblade, the afternoon sun glinting off of it. Then I feel a sting in my left shoulder and I black out for a little bit. I come to. TJ is crying now, still sitting atop me, and making strange animal sounds of his own.

After what seems a whole afternoon has passed, TJ gets pulled up off of me by the bus driver. I hear Miss Howell's voice next to me. I feel pressure on my shoulder, and I can smell cigarette smoke on the driver's clothes and it makes me think of daddy. Why would I think of daddy right now? He would never bring me here. TJ is right. He is a drunk. He never takes me anywhere. Mama would take me anywhere I want, I know, if she could. But she's too busy at her job. So why am I thinking of daddy now? And why did my friend beat me up and stab me? Is this that grown-up stuff mama was crying about? The bus driver lifts me and carries me off away from my classmates who have crowded around. I can hear Miss Howell chatting with him. Her voice sounds faraway and high-pitched. I get another good whiff of cigarette smoke off the driver's shirt. Camels, I think.

Miss Howell has bandaged up my shoulder and set me down in her car. She says that she's taking me to the nearest clinic for stitches, and maybe a shot. Her car smells nice, like her perfume, and she drives really fast, faster than mama. I look out the window and see a string of geese lifting up out of a picked-over cotton field. I want to hold up my binoculars to look at them, but cannot because of the bandage. I wonder what daddy would think of all this. Me with a girlfriend. Me getting attacked by TJ. Me inside my teacher's car speeding towards some clinic for stitches and a shot.

He is probably on his first break right about now, rubbing his back and cursing, lighting up and standing out behind the store. I wonder if he's even thinking of me and how much fun I should be having today. I wonder if he can imagine me with a switchblade knife stuck in my arm. Put there by my best friend. I can just picture him out on that loading dock behind the store. His face puffy from too many Friday night beers. His mouth pursed as if to tell a dirty joke. He is scanning the sky for a high V of geese heading south. I can see him exhaling a big cloud of smoke, and then turning to go back inside to stock the warehouse.

Japanese Fanclub

I'm hand-watering shrubs around the main campus library. Deep into summer semester now. Late July. That arid southwestern heat baking everyone and everything to a mesquite-smoked crisp. While dousing my head and neck with a lukewarm dribble from the hose, I hear Larry, a coworker, beckoning me from across the plaza.

"Ronald!" he shouts. "Dude!" His voice strident and strangely feminine-sounding. "Dude . . . over here!"

My eyes are blurry from sweat and hose water. Across the plaza, Larry appears to me as if in a vision. In his midst are three diminutive women, or maybe teenage girls for that matter. They are all standing beneath a Mexican fan palm, Larry waving frantically and shouting, "Dude!"

I lumber across the plaza to meet Larry's new acquaintances. Upon closer inspection, they are East Asian, Korean or Japanese, attractive, and appear middle-aged. The three of them are dressed identically; cut-off shorts, red Converse hi-tops, straw sunhats, and punk rock black t-shirts — Ramones, Sex Pistols, and The Clash. They bow in tandem to me, and all of a sudden, there's a ringing in my ears. That old tinnitus has returned. I am speechless. I am tired, sweaty, and speechless.

The one in the middle (Ramones) gestures to her left and to her right. "This is Yukiko and Azumi," she says, "and I am Kana." They bow their heads again, and Kana continues, in spot-on English. "You are Ronald? Guitar player and singer for The Chord? We attended your Tokyo concert long ago, and wrote favorably of your show and album in our fanzine." The tinnitus ringing is louder now. Higher-pitched. Oh yes, I know these women. I certainly remember Kana. She hung out backstage with me and seemed interested in spending more time together. I had deflected, as was (and continues to be) my shy and insecure way, so she ended up glomming onto our bassist for that tour.

"You gave us an interview, an exclusive for Japan," Kana continues. "We visited much that week, and your bass player Blaine stayed with me. I bring pictures from then."

I'm standing there in my work clothes, sweat pouring off me, my mouth ajar like some Ozark simpleton.

"Wow," I say. "Uh . . . that's amazing." Larry has stepped off to the side ever so slightly to take this all in. He looks like a kid on Christmas morning, a shit-eating grin smeared across his face.

"Uh...again. Just wow," I stammer. "Of course I remember you all . . ."

I'm feeling light-headed now and can hear the squeal of my Marshall stack feedback. Muffled Japanese applause. *Check one-two. Check one-two . . .*

Kana hands me a long and slender gift-wrapped item. I unwrap it to find a delicate silk print displaying three geishas against a blood-red background. Like an eighth-grade boy having to peel off his T-shirt in gym class, I blush brightly and then find myself bowing to them. "Arigato," I mumble. Out of the corner of my eye, I spy Larry, gobsmacked, astonished by what he's witnessing happen to a coworker.

We all exchange pleasantries for another minute or so, and then I thank them again and apologize for having to return to work. Plans are made to meet up on the weekend. More bowing. *Arigato*. They write down their address in town. *Domo arigato*. Larry and I head back to our dry shrubbery. His face is plastered with amazement and, I think, a touch of pride by proximity to the whole event. He's talking to me and licking his lips and gesticulating, but I cannot hear a word he's saying over that rock-and-roll feedback ringing in my ears.

Growing up in Pinkard, Alabama in the seventies and eighties, counterculture music was just not readily available to the lone, creative soul. One had to put desperate effort into seeking out and finding it, unlike those privileged folks in coastal cities or college burgs. Staticky FM rock picked up via Birmingham or Nashville, glossy guitar magazines featuring hair-metal dumbasses on their covers — that was more the norm for those of us musically inquisitive.

Eventually, a casual campus friend would name-drop someone they knew in a punk band or give the address of an underground record store/head shop in nearby Huntsville or Muscle Shoals. Now, with hindsight, I am somewhat proud of my unhip classic rock upbringing. Those embarrassingly clichéd arena-rock anthems heard on the radio helped me develop my skills with an after-school discipline and obsessive-compulsive attention to technique. That sense of refinement, that becoming of a truly unique artist, came much later on. Too late, in fact, as the pure and vital flames of youth get crassly snuffed out by Cruel Time's wet thumb and index finger.

The Chord came about when I teamed up with Blaine and Howard, a hot rhythm section withering away on Wednesdays and Sundays at some nondenominational strip mall church outside of Pinkard.

The three of us woodshedded that whole summer in Howard's parents' basement. Each of us being inordinately gifted, our sound and collective vibe developed at a frightening pace. The songs dribbled out slowly, however. I was still small-town in heart and mind, a mere babe in the woods concerning "life experience." Blaine, country club handsome to match his name, thumped and stroked upon his Rickenbacker bass and made eyes from stage at every woman in the bar. Howard, sensible and square-headed, kept a steady backbeat and thought more about money than art. You could almost see dollar signs bouncing above him as he clicked the stick-count into each tune. Soon enough, this old high school buddy of Blaine's got us in for an overnight session at Fame Studio in Muscle Shoals. Our EP, *Struck*, was lean and mean and jolted by too much caffeine. The hard stuff came later (again, babes in the woods), alongside lots of guitar effects and sharp popping vocals. I cannot imagine how or why, but for some reason, it got us record label attention out west.

After lunch, Larry is sitting shotgun, spitting snuff into a Wendy's frostie cup. We both work in the university's maintenance department, and are currently headed out to mow those long lawns at the south edge of campus. Larry has known for some time about my sordid musical past, but after just meeting some honest-to-god fans (Japanese no less), he keeps glancing over at me with big puppy dog eyes. I know that he wants to hear more about "that rock star shit," as I've heard him call it before, but I have a diversionary tactic in mind. Fiddling with our truck radio's AM dial, I find some old school Tejano. "Flaco Jimenez," I announce like a drive time DJ. Larry offers up a blank stare. That thumping basso and those bajo sexto chord stabs make a fine solid base for the accordion's happy fluttering to trill upon. Pavlovian, my response to this music. To all music, I reckon. "Suddenly," I say, "I want a shot of tequila with an ice-cold Tecate chaser. Is that racial stereotyping?" Another blank stare from Larry. I continue, "To reduce ethnic music to its corollary imbibables?"

"What?"

"I could write a goddamn doctoral thesis on this subject!" I howl. "Irish trad? Whiskey and stout. Eastern Euro gypsy music? Vodka and a pilsner. Latin American jazz or cumbia? Dark rum over ice. Flamenco? Opera? Cajun? Red wine. It's not rocket science, man!"

My tactic works, and our conversation drifts back to the familiar, the routine, the domestic. He has a new girlfriend, Larry does. A bleached-blonde nightmare from Port Lavaca. I get to hear (and then try to un-hear) such excruciating details concerning the nightly workouts of their genitalia and fingers and lips. Larry lives in a rotting one-bedroom apartment north of campus, a place he calls his "stabbin' cabin." This verbal atrocity alone should disqualify any friendship of ours, but seeing as I'm a live-and-let-live kind of guy, I stick it out with the degenerate. Plus, he's a sweetheart, deep down.

Years ago, on my first visit to his abode (to buy some

acid for the weekend), I'd noticed that Larry's walls were covered with David Lee Roth-era Van Halen posters.

"Hey wow," I said, pointing to Eddie and his stupid striped Kramer ax. I could almost hear that obnoxious distorted finger-tapping noise. "This surely takes me back."

"Hell yeah, man," Larry said. He was literally filling up the galley kitchen with his own prodigious body, all the while pouring shots of Jim Beam for us. "Those fuckers, AC/DC, Blue Oyster Cult. You name them and I've probably seen them in concert."

And then, weakened by blurry camaraderie, my first mistake (or maybe second, after dropping a tab) was to tell Larry about my musical history. His eyes lit up like tiny bonfires. If bourbon was the flammable starter liquid, then my guitar glory story was the struck match. I told him everything.

"Holy shit, man." Larry was on his dumpster dive couch, looking (to my eyes) like some wadded up fast food napkin. He was drunk and high and thoroughly taken aback hearing my rock star biography. Long since faded, of course, but of no matter to him. I had been going on and on for some time about my old band, and I laid it on thick, a veritable one person VH-1 Behind the Music episode. How ahead of our time we were! How misunderstood! How unexpected this angular spiky new wave we unleashed loudly and proudly upon mid-eighties Oak Ridge Boys-assaulted north Alabama. And how we got wise, headed west for a record deal, put our small-town asses out on the road in supporting slots for bigger acts. Theater shows, then arena shows. Our feisty little label in Houston landed us gigs in London, Paris, Amsterdam, Madrid. But the biggest coup by far was one week in Japan.

Our first single was in heavy rotation all over Tokyo FM radio and college stations throughout the country, and their record stores were "moving product," as the suits say.

Larry was practically canine at this point, feral and rabid and hunched on all fours upon the bongwater-stained carpet floor. From somewhere deep down inside his low-hanging hairy gonads, that one true primal question growled upwards. "Pussy?" He moaned. Panting now. Eyes wide open and darting about. "Mmmm . . . grrrr . . . pussy?!"

"Well," I laughed, "none for me as I was spoken for at that time."

Larry cocked his head like that RCA Records dog. This was animal cruelty, surely. Here I was dangling such a potentially exotic story out before him, this Asian sexual chew toy, taunting him with it, and then deciding not to toss it for a game of fetch. I laughed again and said in a mock baby voice, "Who's a good boy?!" At that very moment, the lysergic really kicked in. Larry had indeed become this shaggy mongrel crouched before me. His head still cocked. His Old Yeller eyes locked onto mine. A whining whimpering now just to hear some erotic samurai snatch story.

I sat down beside him and patted his head. "Who's a good boy?" I asked again.

Furry Larry wagged his tail and howled expectantly. His apartment walls had changed from drab gray to a pinkish hue, and they began to bubble and undulate ever so slightly.

It's early Saturday morning, and I'm sipping cold coffee and watching the local weather radar station. A typical midsummer high pressure has settled in, and it won't rain for weeks, maybe a couple of months. I try to wrap my head around the fact that three middle-aged women from Japan have booked a trip over here to track down what's left of my old band. Don't they have careers? Husbands or children to dote upon? Elderly parents to take care of? Jesus, they're still dressed as they were in the early nineties at our concert. I can't figure out if that impresses me, or depresses me.

I pick them up at their hostel east of campus. Same uniforms as yesterday, but different bands. I'm having trouble remembering who's who, so I start referring to them as Ramones, Clash, or Pistols. Except today it's Bauhaus, The Cure, and Devo. I end up just talking with Kana (easy enough to remember), and smiling and nodding at the other two. They've requested a day of thrift store shopping, bowling, and Tex-Mex. I have to politely decline on the bowling (bad hip), which makes them embarrassed and uncomfortable for even bringing it up. Kana frowns and rubs the back of her head furiously. "Sorry," she keeps repeating. "Please forgive." She's acting like she should've already known this little factoid about The Chord lead guitarist, Ronald Tidwell. Like she overlooked some headline in *Melody Maker* back in 1992: Ronnie T, Hot New Wave Shredder, Will Need Hip Replacement By Age 50.

After making a day of it, the four of us end up at El Guapo, my neighborhood go-to cantina for drinks and cheap deep-fried eats. The regular bartender, Esteban, gives me a wink and a nod when we all sit down. "Pigeons coming home to roost, papi," he whispers, "que bueno." All afternoon, the talk has revolved around The Chord, our short time in Japan, influential bands of the past and present, their albums and their live shows, etcetera. I feel like a teenager again, but not in the good way. I feel like these women are ignoring reality, and the ravages of time upon their biological beings. Theirs and mine. I feel like they are stuck in early or even pre-adulthood, and it's starting to bum me out.

Eventually, Kana and I settle in to the personal and the quotidian stuff. I had long forgotten how beautiful she is when she smiles. Of course I had forgotten. It was thirty fucking years ago. She has a daughter attending Yachio University, the very site of our big performance that they attended. Kana has worked many years now in a high-powered Tokyo advertising firm, and thus can afford these long holidays abroad. She and Yukiko and Azumi still attend as many concerts and club shows as they can, I'm guessing like some sad attempt at time travel into their past. I hold back most of my own details, dull as they are, but give a few big ones away. The longtime partner leaving me last year. The guitar school I teach at part-time. The dabbling in Western-style consumer Buddhism. Meditation. Published haiku poems. Then, the full-time university gig with its health benefits. Blah blah blah.

And then in walks Larry, catching us on our second round of tequila shots. Judging from his saloon stagger, he appears to be several rounds ahead of us. His eyes reefer-red and squinted half-shut. I'm guessing that he figured I would bring them here, and I have a feeling that he's going to make a move on any one of them, or (in his dreams) all three. Within minutes, he and Yukiko and Azumi are over at the bar, giggling, snapping selfies, knocking back more shots. Not too shabby, I must admit.

The big conversational bombshell for Kana, I save for

last. "No chance of the band getting back together," I say, shrugging, "obviously." Blaine, our sweet Blaine, wandering soul, suave lady lover, road-dog baying at the heartbroken moon, had taken his own life back in January outside of Nashville. A too-predictable trailer trash ending after all, the son-of-a-bitch. Overdosing on pills in his doublewide's bathtub. Not enough session work? Not enough meaning and purpose in his day-to-day? Who knows? I had been out of touch with him, and also with Howard (busy, yet superfluous in L.A.), for a long time, not out of any trite rock band animosity, but rather, just simple desiccation of unattended-to friendships. This led to guilt, of course, and it had been weighing me down for months now. Like I was walking around with a twenty-pound tumor inside my chest.

Across from me, Kana has started crying, quietly. "Yes," she whispers. "Blaine. I read about that." She dabs with a napkin at her eyes and glances over at her friends laughing it up with Larry. "I'm so sorry." She then pulls a photo from her bag and hands it to me. A beaming beautiful young lady. Long black hair, porcelain skin, piercing blue familiar eyes.

The tinnitus ringing has returned. "Kana," I say, "I've thought often of you over the many years." Bullshit, I think. I just wanted to get laid in Japan, and didn't have the cajones to pull it off. Even with such an impressionable and willing backstage hanger-on. "I always wanted to . . . ."

"Ronald, this is Maki, my daughter," she says, her face wet and finally showing its age. "My daughter. Blaine's daughter . . . ."

For the second time in as many days, I'm speechless. Kana's right hand moves up to cover her trembling mouth, and suddenly she appears to me like some nineteenth century courtesan. The ringing continues, and I swear that the bar's muzak has switched from modern country to koto songs. Raw, anguished, plucked string koto. I then look out the window and see that it's raining somehow. Out of nowhere, apparently, a good soaking subtropical rain shower. I turn back to Kana. "Did he know?"

She suddenly regains her composure, all Eastern formality now. "I never told him," she says. "For his own good." I'm having trouble letting this sink in. Blaine had a daughter he never knew about. In Japan. He had a daughter with a woman who I wanted to be with. The rain is falling heavier now. Improbable, unbelievable, midsummer rain. "No need for him to know," she continues, "I was just thinking of the band, of course."

The ringing stops cold. The koto music in my head stops cold. Larry and the other two are in a hushed conversation now with Esteban. Just the drumming pounding sound of rain. I feel flushed, an anger rising in me. "Thinking of the band?" I ask, a bit louder than I meant to. "Are you fucking kidding me?" Kana flinches for a second, but then resumes her cool pose. I shake my head in disbelief. "Keeping your child from knowing her father? Is music that goddamned important to you?"

Kana flashes me a cold perfunctory smile, and I realize that this is the last we'll see of each other. She grabs her bag and starts sliding over and out of the booth. "Wait," I say, "Wait. I'm sorry about all that." She stops, half-out of her seat, and looks back at me. I clear my throat, bow my head respectfully, and ask again, much softer this time, "Is music really that important to you?" She pauses for a moment, and then brushes tortilla chip crumbs off the front of her Bauhaus t-shirt. Old ghoulish Peter Murphy glares up at me from beneath her small breasts. She rises and goes over to join Larry and her friends at the bar. Within the minute, they are all laughing and clinking shot glasses.

The rain has let up now, so I drop a small stack of crumpled twenties down beside the empty salsa bowls and stand to leave. At the door, I turn back to see Kana at the restaurant's old-school jukebox, flipping through selections. A reverb-drenched boy's choir is erupting from the muzak speakers. The Stones. *You Can't Always Get What You Want.* I look over to find Larry still grinning in his inebriated amazement. He has both arms draped around Yukiko and Azumi, but when he sees me heading out, he grins even bigger and starts yelping like a coyote. He raises both hands up off of the two women, and salutes me with devil horns.

Destination Dollywood

The inevitable titty joke always disgusted me. Be it in the locker room, the parking lot, the church retreat, etcetera. I mean, we've all heard them, and heard them all, right? And what red-blooded American boy did *not* want to cuddle up in her lap and suckle upon those gigantic Smoky Mountain paps? No one that I knew of in Tishomingo County. So yes, forget the ample bosom, the cascading blonde waves. It was that angelic east Tennessee voice in my headphones. In my dreams. Those songs, that voice, transcending mere teenage thrusting lust and enrapturing me into a pure pathos beyond my years. Jolene. Heartbreaker. I Will Always Love You. We've heard them all, right?

And so it came to pass that I fell upon hard times with wife number three, and thus left Corinth in a pill haze and with a sense of impending biblical doom. Each daytime sky seemed infrared and harmful to my pupils. I stayed indoors at the Motel 6 on I-40 near Bucksnort, only coming out at night to scavenge like a raccoon the convenience stores and yogurt shops. In December rain some pimply fellow outside TCBY handed me a tract from his church in Jackson. I took it to my mildewed room and read it over and over in bed until dawn. A Big Gulp un-gulped on the nightstand. QVC on the televison. Here you come again, Lord. Wrap my heart around your little finger.

Jesus brought me peace. Jesus brought me home. Jesus brought me back to Dolly.

Early days, well before the hormonal *sturm und drang*, I was a towheaded lad on tippy toes dropping my letter into the outgoing mail slot at the main street post office. Daddy standing by, grinning. His friend Hal behind the counter grinning, chewing on an unlit stogie. Into the bin fell a fan letter from me to Miss Parton. I had no address other than — "Nash Vill, Ten" — or some such snot-nosed trailer park nonsense. Needless to say, the letter went undelivered, I'm sure, and unanswered, I know. Not hearing back over the years just made me love her more. Of course it did, as her songs would seem to say.

So after all those pills and booze and Slim Jims and motel sex, sweet Jesus helped me get my shit together. I attended night classes at the trade school in Corinth and became interested in aviation. I even befriended a finance instructor who also sang bass in our church choir. Alan knew of my plight, and appreciated all the effort in bettering myself. He had flown crop dusters as a young man over in Alabama, low and reckless above the high cotton. One evening after accounting class he told me about a new flight simulator up in Memphis. I could get us both in if you're interested, he said.

Interested wasn't exactly the right word. *Beckoned, called, drawn* to like some hairy white moth to the oil drum flame.

We made good time through that Highway 72 peckerwood traffic, then on into the big city to find ourselves inside the cool quiet sawed-off cockpit hull of some Boeing or other. Alan joked with the attendants as we settled in for our simulation flight. Can I check my email on this thing, he smirked, ha ha. He dialed us up a run from Memphis International direct to Dulles. Sure, throw in some fat thunderheads over Kentucky while you're at it. Our seats shook like real upon takeoff, and soon enough lightning was sparking on the far eastern horizon as we leveled off at 36,000 feet.

Alan had to take a call on his cell. He spun backwards in his seat and started arguing with his wife over weekend plans or the like. I was left to my own devices with a shining multitude of heavenly buttons and switches. All blinking and just waiting to be pinched or diddled. The simulator screen was displaying Bowling Green off to our left and Knoxville to our right. Alan stood up out of his pilot's chair, groaning and shouting now into his phone. Not now Helen, he yelled, now is not a good time! He stepped off the hull, screaming into his phone and walking across the hangar towards the staff exit.

I had taken the steering apparatus and veered off towards those voluptuous Appalachian mounds poking up from below. O such a landscape for lick and caress! Lenoir City, Maryville, Gatlinburg, Pigeon Forge. And right there before me lay my beloved, my unknowable, my Dolly, embodied by her saccharine sweet sacrilegious theme park.

This was far better than any pill or powder or motel sex or Christ himself! My hands now sweaty with lust, with ape rage, I throttled forward and down, deep down, hard and fast into such the tender absolute love awaiting me below. My seat shook as if in an earthquake. Red lights flashing. Dollywood now very real and filling up the screen.

I found out the hard way and I'm never going to break your heart.

Guess I had to go away just to find what I'd left behind.

You're the only one. You're the only one.

Take me back to where we started from.

Preacher Down

Ican still picture his body crumpled upon the parsonage floor, the refrigerator door left open for some reason. Blood everywhere. A large pool of it bright red and viscous. I was meeting him there just that morning to discuss an upcoming book drive, and oh my god! I'm sorry. Give me a moment. You don't mind the flask, do you? I need a sip or two to steady my hands. Calm whatever nerves haven't frayed beyond mending. Such the nightmare vision that is burned like a brand onto my brain! I see it right before I drift off into my restless sleep. I see it first thing every morning since. Sweet Brother Bruce reduced to a pile of cold gray meat spoiling upon the kitchen floor.

Do I sound a tad cynical? Bitter? Well, it was, after all, these pious privet hedge-pruning prudes with their gossipy little circle jerk Bible study groups who eventually did the poor man in. What with their sneaking around, with their slippery slander, they may as well have loaded the shotgun for him and propped it up beneath his quivering chin.

He came to us from Tennessee, this much I remember. Not with any walking tall bravado, or snuff dipping, or spitting of chaw. Not even sporting that silly Charlie Daniels beard fashionable around these parts at the time. No, this fellow was meek and mild. A veritable lily of the fields. His voice was as Christ's own, whispering to each and every one of us — *wake up. Wake up.* His soft, lilting mountain brogue. His tiny hands folded upon the pulpit like two mourning doves at roost. His eyes (quick to avert!) both blue and gray. A sadness of Shiloh in the color. Of Chickamaugua.

Brother Bruce, we called him. From old Bryce family stock, still propagating and feuding in those hilly Cumberlands east of Nashville. Bryces were not known for their Christian charity, or *agape* love. Shoot first and what's a question? That would be the Bryce way. Brother Bruce must've descended direct from heaven to walk amongst and interact with such unwashed heathenry.

He had latched onto a few likeminded souls while attending seminary in northern Kentucky. C.S. Lewis-types. Philosophers. Sensitive readers of classical poetry. He grew somewhat comfortable inside his thin little husk of humility and blossomed, as it were, from out of the dusty books and cool darkened knaves. The Word of God itself is bold! He reasoned. It is revolutionary! Therefore, he need not be. The Word speaks for itself.

I for one welcomed this highbrowed theologian to our backwater little church. Pinkard, Alabama is an odd place for some brightly colored bird to show up, I will admit.

We (the town majority, rather, not I) prefer the hellfire shouting kind, to be honest, and do not trust soft-spoken reason, even notated by chapter and verse. The parishioners played their predictable parts by sniffing around him at all times, just waiting for something elitist or fey or too *outré* for their so-called community standards. Maybe a stray mention of liberation theology? Christ as a radical? Love thy enemy? My heavens! Call the authorities! Get a rope!

Therefore, I had the distinct honor and pleasure of working alongside Brother Bruce as the church librarian (mostly mornings; afternoons I sketch the geese in Spring Park). My name is Herbert, but I'm really no concern to you. Folks here call me Herb and for the most part leave me be. I also am quiet and bookish. I sleep on a cot in a back corner of the church basement, and proudly serve Our Lord in my own private and odd way. Odd meaning *unusual*, and private meaning *none of your damn business*. I maintain a small collection of Methodist history, philosophy, and ephemera, available at all times for any townsperson here wishing to broaden their dull and narrow minds.

I had not the slightest idea of any unhappiness or suffering on his part, at least not until near the very end. I do seem to recall a wincing look that would flash across his face from time to time right in the middle of conversation. Weather, local sporting events, it didn't matter what was being said. It was if some past life pain was inflicting itself incrementally on the dear fellow. And also this, unfortunately: his breath of late had reeked rankly and deeply of firewater. I know, I know, I'm not one to talk, as you see me here blurry-eyed, with hands trembling. But Brother Bruce was supposedly a teetotaler, no doubt in reaction to his Bryce family's epically debauched history, and he'd led our congregation stone cold sober for going on two years. Actually, the first time I detected that sour mash scent (late on a Thursday evening as he helped me sort through new hymnals), I felt even more endeared to him, if that was possible. The poor man! How I would love to have poured him three fingers of my finest Irish malt, clink glasses like a couple of Oxford types in their corner pub! Old J.R.R. and C.S. pontificating on the wonders of language and civilization, the vastness of Creation.

But what happened was, one of those privet hedge prudes in the congregation had also caught wind of his tippler's breath. Their sniffing around became more akin to snorting and huffing, and then baying like autumn coonhounds. A few bold voices even brought it up at a Wednesday night meeting. It seemed the villagers had grabbed their pitchforks and lit their torches and set out to dispatch of the monster. Poor Brother Bruce had no idea what was coming for him. Not even the senseless Old Testament violence of his own Tennessee clan background could prepare him for such the calamity, such the proprietary back stabbing awaiting him in the church office that very next morning.

I was away at the time, feeding geese at the aforementioned Spring Park and sketching them with shaky hands. A whole flock was parading past on the opposite bank of the creek. I noticed one tiny gosling had dropped far behind his siblings, and the mother circling back to honk and flap and chastise him. Poor bastard. Should I have stayed back to defend Brother Bruce's honor? Be his Mother Goose? Let ye without sin cast the first stone, and all that? Of course I should have. But, realizing that I loved him too much to cause embarrassment, I slipped away beforehand. In a gray trench coat I sat on my park bench, nipping at some Irish, scribbling postmodern bird forms into my art pad.

Later on, Bruce told me the news. "The church elders want me gone," he said. "As soon as possible." I was stacking service bulletins on my desk, shocked somehow even with the inevitability of it all. I kept my back to him so as to hide wet eyes. He cleared his throat. "Did you hear me?"

I turned slowly, letting him view my fallen face. "They are a vile and simple species, Brother Bruce," I replied. "They...we, don't deserve you." My eyes lowered to the floor.

"I thought I was following the honorable path," he said. "God's will and all that . . . ."

Mysterious ways? I suddenly thought. He seemed to hear my mind.

"Oh, I know how the Lord works, dear Herb. Or at least I used to *believe* that I knew how the Lord works." He pulled a bulletin from the stack and glanced at it for a few seconds. "Nowadays I've realized that I'm just peddling mythology. Boogeyman stories. Throwing hand shadows on the cave walls. Browbeating my fellow villagers with Stone Age wisdom. Scaring them, guilting them into hankering for some make-believe paradise." He then crumpled the bulletin and tossed it to my desk.

I continued staring at the floor, speechless, and after a long pause I looked up to find him gone.

That evening, I came calling to the parsonage, hoping to find my preacher in a lighter and more accepting mood. I had also planned a goodbye speech, as it were. My heart was simply broken. The attraction I felt for him was in no sense sexual, but the flashing intensity of it did make me question who I was, exactly, and what sort of man I was supposed to be.

Approaching his door, I could hear heavy metal music thudding from inside. Strangely cathartic, even aggressive, I thought. Wrestling with his demons, maybe? I knocked loudly a couple of times until he opened up.

He stood before me, shirtless and hairy-chested, hoisting a double-barrel shotgun. Black Sabbath blazing away from his hi-fi in the corner. The very same hi-fi I had heard only Brahms or Handel on, and at low volume. My face displayed shock, and Brother Bruce snorted laughter and shouted "Sorry! Forgot I had this." He placed the gun upon his kitchen table, then scrambled towards the stereo to turn down Sabbath. As he leaned over to tweak the volume, I couldn't help but notice his lat muscles rippling, and I wondered how one developed such things while hunched over in a library cubicle reading ancient translations of Aramaic.

I sat on his sofa and listened as he ran through a litany of petty grievances and passing annoyances. Small towns. Smaller minds. Why had he not followed his heart and moved to a big city? "So much loneliness and confusion there," he cried. "So much vibrancy in the variety of sins. Such the turnover rate in a needy, half-vagrant congregation!" He had missed his calling, he surmised, and ended up in a stagnant, swampy pool of cultural and spiritual cessation. He had settled for a steady paycheck. He had lost sight of Love, and settled instead for Lucre.

I had nothing to say. My mind was blank from his southern gothic shock and awe and I mumbled, "mmm," and "of course" as he paced back and forth and opened up his heart. Half an hour into his diatribe, I realized he had still not put on a shirt. His physique seemed sculpted as if by some ancient Greek, and I flushed in my face and glanced back towards the kitchen table shotgun.

"Oh Herb," he muttered, "I'm just driving up to see my folks tomorrow. Duck hunting with daddy and all that."

"Mmm . . . of course . . . ."

Brother Bruce came forward and grasped my hands. "Thank you, Herb, for being such a true friend. I'll never forget this."

We hugged. I inhaled my friend's musky Tennessee scent, and swear that I blacked out for a short time just standing there in his embrace. My goodbye speech lost to the ether. I came to, and in my heart of hearts I knew this would be the last time I saw him. And also, the last time he would see or speak to anyone. I realized all this this while pulling away from his sweaty chest. It was clear to me that he had no hunting trip planned. No homecoming visit the next day with his parents. For all I knew, they were both long deceased, and he was planning on joining them. I wiped my eyes and stared down at the yellow parquet floor. Every other tile had a cross pattern in them, and from my vantage point all of the crosses were inverted. Had Brother Bruce ever noticed this unintentional blasphemy? I wondered. I felt as if I would black out again, but I steadied myself, and all I recall after that is his door closing softly behind me. I stumbled somehow back to my sad cot in a daze, and lay there for hours, shaking, suspecting what that dear fellow was going to do. And yet, I talked myself out of this gut hunch. I even tried to pray. Really! I wasn't exactly sure what to ask for, though. Thy will be done? What the hell does that mean? Isn't that just a catchall explanation of Fate? The Lord's Will. It Was Meant To Be. Jesus Called! Eventually, I tired of this and drifted off into a deep black dreamless sleep, only to awaken to the nightmare of the next morning. I swear to you that this is true, all of it, but I honestly could care less if you don't believe me. Because — fuck you. Fuck all of you. Who gives you the right to judge? Privet-hedge pruning prigs! Simple-minds! Back-stabbers! I've packed my meager possessions to go, and I'll never darken these doors again. There is no judgment anyway. No right or wrong. No Almighty. We are all just scuttling beach crabs tossed about in the swirling surf.

And yet some people shine like shooting stars in the night. A rare few! So simple yet miraculous how they streak and flame out above. Any of us are lucky to behold them, much less follow in their path. These gifted ones burn quick and bright and show the rest of us groveling apes what a heaven might look like. A fleeting glimpse of eternity. But they fade fast. They fade and fall, leaving us all to turn our tired backs upon the mystery.

Why Standest Thou Afar, O Lord?

The telephone is ringing. I drop the casserole dish in the backyard and waddle up the porch steps. On the seventh ring I pick up, my voice dry and raspy from that biting north wind. "Hello?"

"Mama Libby, it's Foy."

Foy is a decent enough son-in-law. He gives instruction in choral and classical music over at the State Teacher's College, yet seems to possess the mind of a nine-year-old. Crew-cutted, whip-thin, he dresses neat and tidy, if not a bit foppish, and exhibits the nervous nature of some agitated tropical bird. My youngest, Evelyn, fell for him a few years back. It must've been all that hushed talk at the soda shop about Romantic-era operas and such. They married, moved over to College Town, and now have a baby girl named Belle.

I pull off my toboggan, flecked with melting snowflakes, and set it down on the kitchen table. "Almost didn't make it to the phone," I say. "Just putting the last of the Christmas dressing down for the redbirds and sparrows. They're out there by the bunches. It's already snowing here ... how about you all?"

A short pause filled with the sound of a baby crying.

45

"What? No, not yet." Coughing sounds in the background. "Listen . . . Belle is awful sick. High fever and sweats. Hacking her little head off. We think it might be the croup."

"Oh my," I say. "Bless her sweet heart. You got her wrapped up? You saying your prayers?"

"Yes, ma'am. But Ev and I need some help, I reckon." A long pause, then more hacking coughs in the background. "Would you mind spending a few days in town?"

My heart sinks a bit. Who will kiss the framed photo of Henry at midnight tonight? A good husband of thirty-five years, Henry was, even though he occasionally got ornery after a sip or two. Who will lay peacefully in my bed with the Good Book and listen to all the creaks and pops of this old house settling into a new year? Who will feed these redbirds and sparrows in this cold spell? As the hymn says — His Eye Is On The Sparrow, but I swear, the longer I live, the more I seem to think He can't see everything.

Glancing out the window, I notice the snow picking up, blurring the backyard. Male redbirds fall from bare branches into the tray feeder like drops of blood from a wound. "You'll have to come get me, Foy. You know I don't drive."

Another long silence, then the baby coughing, Evelyn speaking low in the background. Foy replies with the sound of a man being pulled from a baptizing river, sputtering and gasping for sweet summer air. "I'll be there soon as I can."

An hour and a half later Foy pulls up in his silly looking German car. The only one like it in town, he always says. He bought it last year in Birmingham and on the way home stopped at a service station to fill up and the attendant couldn't find the gas tank. I think it looks like a clown car from Barnum and Bailey. My next-door neighbor Lloyd says it's, and I quote, a damn Nazi car. But it's bright green and Evelyn likes it, so who cares what I think? The thing belches and farts gray smoke into my front yard. Foy jumps out, leaving his door open, the lights on.

"Thank you Libby!" he shouts over the engine noise. "I just don't know what to do . . . Ev is real nervous and jumpy around Belle." He forgot to put on his overcoat or a hat and he's standing in the slushy driveway with that hard north wind whipping about. "I mean, she's got her wrapped up good. Keeps checking on her fever. But I think we both just need your steady hand. Someone with a deeper faith."

I take a long look at the front of my house. I've never noticed that it has the appearance of some drunken holiday sad face. The two darkened windows droop like sleepy eyes, the door a fat gin blossom nose, the icy stoop frowns like a pair of wind-chapped lips.

Be a good Christian, Libby, I tell myself. This is your flesh and blood we're talking about.

The road stays wet until we get up into the hills near Littleville. The higher we go, the whiter the highway lanes become. Foy is fidgety, his right hand moving off the steering wheel every so often to touch his wallet, his shirt pocket checkbook, his eyeglasses case beside the gearshift. He taps the brakes, speeds up, taps the brakes, speeds up.

Out my window, Hawk Pride Mountain squats east of the highway, snow dusting the slash pines and cedars on its ridgetop. My Henry was raised on the eastern slope of Hawk Pride. A little hamlet called Dropoff. Not even a hamlet, I guess, more like a coal miner's compound of a half-dozen or so rickety shacks perched among the stony outcroppings. Just as stony was Henry's daddy, a hard man, black-lunged and godless. There was, in fact, a Bible in the house, their only book. But neither Henry nor his daddy could read. I reckon they used it to squash cockroaches, or as a doorstop. Whenever company came calling, Henry's daddy would ask of them to read a bit from it, just to pass the time if nothing else. The visitor, a cousin or a neighbor of some sort, would inevitably turn to the Old Testament, what with its begatting and murders and plagues. This all sounded about right to Henry's daddy, and he had of late taken up the notion that if there really was a God somewhere up in the sky, he was pretty sure the crazy son-of-a-bitch didn't care much for him or anybody else. In the meantime, young Henry was driven like a ginny mule. He helped pull up coal. He hunted squirrel and quail and possum for supper. He tended the thin-soiled garden his mother would have tended, had she lived. After her death, Henry's daddy took turns courting her younger sisters, eventually running them all off to Mississippi or someplace else. All of this must've weighed heavy on young Henry. The women coming and going, the mason jar being passed around, the shotgun always loaded and nearby, the sudden and senseless sickness and violence. Old Testament, all of it. Of course Henry would end up in the mines. Of course he was ornery about God. Of course he had his daddy's mean streak, a mile wide and twice and long.

Foy steers us one-handed up and over a hilly pass, tapping the brakes, speeding up. "Hon," I say, "lay off the brakes in this ice. That's what Cousin Jimmie tells us to do. He works up at that big tractor plant in Iowa. Slow it down before this bad curve up here." He eases off the gas and we coast along gently, taking the curve with ease. We haven't seen another pair of headlights in ten minutes or so. Most folks are staying put. Most folks have more sense than we do.

There's a bit more traffic once we get into town, but not much. As soon as we've parked on the street in front of their redbrick apartment building, Evelyn leans out through an upstairs screen door and yells, "Mama, thank you for doing this."

In the time it took Foy to come get me, the snow started falling here and is now ankle-deep. The metal stairs up to their apartment are thick with ice. "It's OK, hon. Let's just get that little one on the mend." I slip on the very first step. "Y'all haven't put in an elevator yet?" Foy takes my right hand in his and we slowly ascend to the second floor.

Their apartment is the size of an outhouse and summerhot. I can hear Baby Belle coughing from back in the bedroom like some tiny backwoods bootlegger. Evelyn is floating down the hallway towards us. She seems scared as a schoolgirl and yet somehow detached from it all. Her clothes have the wrinkled appearance of having been on her body for several days.

"Ev," says Foy, "go get some rest now. We'll watch over Belle for awhile."

Evelyn cocks her head as if she's heard jingle bells on the rooftop. She stares up at the hallway cobwebs and blurts out "Ain't Marnie called a little while ago!" Aunt is pronounced *ain't*, not *ant* or *ahnt*. Marnie is as it looks. "Says since Libby is coming up she's on her way over to visit . . . ."

"Jesus no!" honks Foy, his lightly-stubbled face falling

apart like a wet paper bag. "Call her back and tell her to stay home! Is she crazy?"

In fact, yes, my youngest sister Marnie is crazy. Crazy as a goddamn loon. Lord forgive me for taking Your Holy Name in vain, but I must emphasize the point being made. She's what my dear Henry would, and did, refer to as batshit-crazy.

I seem to recall Big Mamo dropping her when she was still a little thing. She hit the edge of the cradle, bounced off a padded armchair, then plopped onto the hardwood floor. That could explain her being just a tad "off". That and the fact that it runs in the family, straight to us from the dank bogs of Ireland.

Or this — when the weather was nice, Big Mamo would get her guitar and a neighbor would come over with his mandolin and we'd all sit out on the porch. *Pretty Polly. Barbara Allen. Will Sweethearts Know Each Other There?* Mamo had a voice rough as pine bark, but her high notes rang pitch-perfect and clear. All of us would sit quiet and still in wonder. All of us except for little Marnie. She'd be down the steps at the edge of where the porch bulb cast its weak light, grabbing at lightning bugs just to squash them in her hands. That was Marnie, even as a little girl; taking pretty lights from the night sky just to extinguish them forever.

Or how about this — several years back Marnie opened a beauty salon on Main Street in College Town. She catered towards church wives and grandmothers, but would take in just about anyone who needed some attention. One day a dapper gentleman comes strolling in and asks for a haircut. Marnie recognizes this man to not only be an old flame from school, but someone who stood her up once, and later mocked her before a crowd at the church social. She proceeds to seat him, all business-like, and wraps up his neck and shoulders for a trim. In a flash, she grabs a can of kerosene, for her heater, and then douses the gentleman's neck, massaging it in good. Right about the time he's gotten a whiff, noticing it's not some Parisian styling product, she's touched her lit cigarette to the back of his neck. Lit up like a bonfire, the man lurches out of his chair and runs screaming onto the sidewalk. A next-door neighbor happened to be watering his lawn and was able to douse the fire quick enough, with only minor burns to the man's head and neck. Marnie was taken in, but got off by telling the judge she'd made an honest mistake, and had thought she was grabbing styling product, the Parisian kind, because the gentleman was indeed of the dapper sort, and he seemed worthy of it. It also didn't hurt that this particular judge had once carried a torch for Marnie, and he now vowed to see her at least once a week for a stylish touch-up in the back, and on the sides.

"Ev," I say, "Don't worry about Marnie. We'll visit for awhile, then I'll send her on her way." Foy grunts and heads down the hall to check on Belle. "By the way, how'd she sound?"

Evelyn slowly rubs her eyes with thumb and index finger. I'm just about to repeat the question when she says, "Fine, I guess. She said 'good afternoon' when I answered. It was eight-thirty or so this morning. You think she's OK?"

"That sounds about right, Ev. Like I said, I'll take care of her. Don't worry about it." We both glance out their living room window, the curtains parted slightly from when

Evelyn was peeking out for Foy and myself. The snow has really picked up. I believe even Cousin Jimmie up in Iowa would be impressed. A horn honks on the street below, a door slams. "Good afternoon!" a voice booms up through the cold air.

"Gird your loins," says I.

Marnie enters the apartment like some gusty winter blast. She's toting an armful of covered dishes and she's not wearing an overcoat in this weather, just her black Sunday dress with a bright red shawl around the shoulders. "New Year's Eve gift!" she yelps, then laughs. "Blizzard conditions out there...my truck was skidding all over the place." Her hair and shawl are soaking wet and she's hacking her pack-a-day cough. From down the hall, Baby Belle wakes up and answers with coughs of her own. Call and response, like old field hands.

"Leftover cheese straws for everyone," says Marnie. Between Thanksgiving and Christmas she churns out boxes and boxes of cheese straws, as well as rum-soaked fruitcakes, for folks all over town. Makes a pretty penny at it as well. "These aren't quite stale yet. I added more pepper this year!"

Evelyn takes the covered dishes back into the kitchen, a look of pale exhaustion plastered to her pretty face. "You didn't have to bring goodies, Marnie," I say. "This isn't exactly a family reunion here."

Marnie unwraps herself from the wet shawl and cuts a quick glance at me. "It's good to see you too, sis." Hands on wide hips, she spreads a smirk, her eyes blinking slow like a lizard's.

"Now Marnie, don't be that way." I take her shawl and lay it on the back of a chair. "Ev and Foy just need a little moral support here, not a New Year's Eve party. We all need to pray and plead the blood of Jesus and get this little girl healed."

She lets loose a loud staccato cough, Marnie does, a quick explosion of phlegm. "Taken her to a doctor yet?" she croaks. A hand snakes into her purse for a you-know-what.

"Hon, you're not gonna smoke in here. Out on the balcony in the blizzard, if you must." Marnie snaps the purse shut. "No doctor yet," I say. "She's wrapped up and in bed. Holy Spirit'll take care of the rest."

"Huh," Marnie grunts. She grabs up the shawl and wraps it around her damp hair. Placing the unlit cigarette between her fat lips, she opens the door to the balcony. "There's a nice new hospital up in town now. I passed it on the way over . . . ."

Back in the tiny bedroom, the three of us hold hands and stand around Baby Belle. For the moment she isn't coughing, peaceful, lightly sleeping with a slight fever. Ev and Foy look like a pair of deer in some hunter's headlights. Ev's slender hand trembles in mine, childlike. Marnie comes in from her smoke and lurches over in the corner. I take in a deep breath to begin the intoning, the beseeching. My lungs fill with her mentholated stink.

"O Heavenly Father!" I holler. "Hear us at this time. We offer up to you sweet little Baby Belle, who is sick and in need of Your healing grace!" From the corner I hear a crunching sound. My right eye flicks open to spy Marnie stuffing her wrinkled face with stale cheese straws. With her other hand, she flicks through a magazine. I start to say something, but instead let it slide. Deep breath . . . then another deep breath.

I continue on. "We plead the blood of Jesus for this child to be healed!" Foy hawks up something in his throat. "Hallelujah," he mumbles. Ev gives my hand a quick squeeze and I hear her sniffling. The power of prayer can bring tender souls to tears, I've always found. "Blessed be the name of the Lord! Amen." We drop hands and open our eyes. The room seems a bit brighter, feels a bit warmer. Marnie steps forward, brushing crumbs off her chest. "Amen!" she shouts. "What was her temp the last time you checked?"

Evelyn snugs up the sheets around Belle. "Down to 101, I believe. I should check again but she's sleeping awfully nice. It's been awhile since she's coughed . . . ."

A loud pop from down the street and the bedroom lamp goes out. The room is suddenly dark as a tomb, and little Belle wakes up on queue with a sharp hack. "Oh!" yells Ev. "Is that the electricity?" Foy grabs his overcoat in the hall and heads for the door. Marnie parts a curtain and stairs out at an evening sky heavy with snow. Is she enjoying this? Is that silly smirk back on her face? I'll slap it right off, I tell myself.

"Ev, go get us some candles lit," I say. "Marnie? You put on a pot of coffee. I'll grab us some extra quilts and we can ring in the New Year by candlelight." When they leave the room, I lean over croupy little Belle and whisper, "We'll keep you warm, sweet one."

Foy comes in later looking like the abominable snowman. "It's up to my knees by now," he says. "Never seen anything like it." He pantomimes the current state of a big red oak down near the corner of Main, its thick middle section split in two, half of it on a bungalow's roof and the other half in the road with power lines popping underneath. "Looks like we'll be without electricity for awhile," he says. "And you can forget about driving back, Marnie. Nobody's out on the roads now."

I can't stand it when he gets this way. "Foy hon, please sit down and take some rest." He's pacing up and down the hallway and peeking in on Belle at every pass. Candles flicker on the kitchen table, throwing a weak light throughout the apartment. Foy keeps pacing, casting a long grotesque shadow on the ceiling each time he nears our end of the hall. A Lon Chaney Bela Lugosi-type shadow. Marnie slurps her coffee. She takes it black and would be chain-smoking, I know, so this must be a bit trying for her. Instead, I hear her chuckling.

"What's so funny?" I ask in a whisper. Ev has just nodded off on their ratty little couch.

Marnie meets my stare. "Seems more like Halloween here than New Year's Eve." She chuckles again. "That candlelight and those spooky prayers of yours. And now here comes Count Dracula up the hallway . . . Lord, somebody get him a nerve pill!"

"Sis," says I. "Just be nice and let us handle this our way." Marnie's crooked smile fades. She sets down her coffee and rises to her feet. "Your way ain't the only way, Libby," she says, smoothing out the front of her dress. "If you don't mind, I'll take first watch with Belle. Y'all catch a nap if you can."

She plods down the hallway with a couple of extra quilts. Foy has finally settled down and is lightly snoring at Evelyn's feet. The two of them sport the glowing faces of children, tired from play and innocent in a deep winter slumber.

Even after several cups of coffee, I have dozed off. In my

dream, all four of us have taken Belle out to the city park by the river in College Town. A hot sun hangs up high and lazy in a brilliant blue sky. Goldfinches flit and warble in the tall oaks. Little Belle is in her Easter dress, bright pink, with a cheery bonnet on top. She's several years older, all towheaded curls and fussiness. The rest of us seem the same age, maybe even younger. Suddenly, Big Mamo appears beneath a sweetgum tree. She pulls her guitar out of a croker sack and starts tuning up. We all hold hands and start singing, shape notes at first, led by Mamo. Then I lead us in a few choruses of *Will The Circle Be Unbroken?* Belle takes off running and does loops around the sweetgum. The goldfinches from the tall oaks fly over and light on the sweetgum branches right above Belle. They start in with their warbling, Belle giggling, her hair glowing in the summer sun. Foy grabs his baritone tuba, toots a few warm-up notes, then announces a musical piece by Ravel, intricate and devilish with its odd time and sixty-fourth note trills. When, mercifully, it's over, he tosses the brass contraption into the river and we all watch it float away. Marnie picks up Belle, places her on a merry-go-round and gives it a push. Foy and Ev hold hands off to the side, cooing like springtime doves. Belle claps and squeals as the great rusted wheel starts spinning faster, faster. I try to speak but cannot. Marnie takes a few steps back, spreads her hands out like a preacher, and begins laughing her deep fruity laugh. Stop it Marnie, I try to say. Sssss . . . sssss . . . my lips are stitched shut, tongue fat and useless in my mouth. The merry-go-round lifts out of the ground. Still spinning, it floats upwards, taking the giggling little girl over the oaks, over the goldfinches, up to the sun . . . .

I'm awakened by the front door clicking open. My

vision is blurry, but I can make out Marnie. She's outfitted with Foy's overcoat and has a thick-quilted bundle under her left arm. From deep inside it, I hear a tiny cough. "Don't you dare wake them," she hisses at me, an index finger pressed to her lips, keys dangling from her hand. "Her fever's up and she needs a damn doctor." The door is halfway open and behind her I see that it's finally stopped snowing.

"Marnie," I whisper, starting to get up from my chair. "Wait . . . ."

She quietly shuts the door behind her. I settle back down, trying to make sense of what I've just seen. My head is heavy, still groggy from slumber. Maybe I'm still asleep.

Foy and Ev are both snoring, huddled together on the couch. Is this still some dream? Where's the summer sun, the tall oaks, the merry-go-round? Is this the Lord working in His mysterious way? I try to imagine what my dear Henry would do, but cannot. On his deathbed he had said — Thy will be done. Whose will, I wonder. Wasn't he just replaying a scene from his youth? A neighbor reading the Bible aloud, Henry sitting at the table, still and respectful, his daddy drunk and wheezing in the corner. Would he have bundled up a sick child and hauled ass through a snowstorm to the hospital? I don't rightly know what he would've done tonight. Sometimes I can't remember what his voice sounded like. Sometimes I'm not sure if he even existed at all. Henry or God, take your pick. I lay my head back and shut my eyes. So tired. I'm so tired. Thy will be done . . . .

Heavenly Father, I begin, but no other words come. I should pray, I know. But maybe I'll just slip back into that sweet dream. Did You see her way up there, giggling and spinning with all those little goldfinches? Did You hear us below, praising You with song? Heavenly Father, do You hear our prayers? Do You see our dreams?

Before drifting off, I catch the sound of a truck cranking. It revs high a couple of times, then the crunching sound of tires spinning in snow. On the fourth rev, it clears the curbside drift. I listen to it slowly hum down the street, taking a right onto Main.

The Happy Hitters
Sing Songs of
Praise

My name is Lonnie Sherrill and I pick guitar for our Lord and Savior Jesus Christ. Pick the hell out of it. I tear into them damn strings like I'm pumping well water on a summer afternoon or beating off behind the barn. It's a fine Martin on loan from our high tenor, Otho. He purchased it in Cullman last summer but can't play worth a shit. I took it up and haven't set it down since. My calluses are a source of pride down at the general store where I work, and Eunice tells me I thrash about and flex fingers deep in sleep.

A cold autumn Wednesday night prayer meeting with us leading the worship. Otho stands back beside the piano now where his brother Dale sits to play. Oakman First Baptist Church. Walker County. Otho croons high and lonesome as Dale drones bass notes and pokes at the keys like a child sick on cough syrup. Dale saw action in the Pacific while Otho was skipped over on account of his crooked right arm. Crooked from a horse bucking.

HAROLD WHIT WILLIAMS

Crooked enough for him not to make this fine Martin sing like I do.

Pleading the blood of Jesus here in Oakman. Lord God Almighty, can we sing! The Happy Hitters, we're called, and those backwoods and small town congregations eat us up and holler out for more. They jitter and shake and cluck their thick tongues in a Holy Spirit trance. On this particular evening we've wound down our set for their preacher and his altar call. Folks meekly coming forward to be born again. Backsliders. Cotton farmers and roughneck miners. A housewife showing off pretty legs in her new Sears & Roebuck dress. As we pack up afterwards, I catch Otho sneaking peeks at his guitar, *my* guitar now, with eyes drooping like a newborn kitten's. He is overly tall, buzz-cutted and weak-chinned, and pretty much lets the world and its inhabitants have its way with him. As a stringy young fellow, his family sent him out to Arizona one summer with TB, that high and dry air being thought of as a curative. He came back east without his croup, but permanently pink and spindly like some rare desert plant.

Halfway to Tuscaloosa now and all in need of a great piss. Our front man Clyde pulls us over beside a low flat sad pasture. There is heavy hoar frost on the knee-high roadside fescue and our streams are steaming up the night air around us. Clyde pops off a couple of poots and shouts, "Sweet Jesus that Martin sounds good in your hands, Lon!"

I give it a shake and zip up. "Thanks chief," I say, cutting my eyes over to Otho hunched over in his water-making. "Nice of the Big O to let me borrow it."

Clyde squints hard, then wheezes, "Is it though?"

"Uh, well . . . ."

"Seems to me like it fits just so right there in your paws. Whereas he can't fret worth a flitter to save his damn life."

Otho lumbers between us, slumped and red-faced, back to the car.

"Meant to be, Lon," says Clyde, "meant to be."

Early Monday morning at the general store and I'm amongst the dusty sacks of flour and sugar with my clipboard and pencil and my reading glasses dangling down when Otho strolls up before me with a whispered "hey."

"Big O," says I. " Can't get enough of me, huh?" Clyde had dropped me home first in the wee hours last night after our big tent revival singing up in Russellville, so I know that Otho got less sleep than I did. And I got very little. "Eunice might get jealous, O. You got some sugar in your pocket for me? Ha!"

Otho half-smiles, his kitten eyes drooping. "That's a good one, Lon. Can I use that on my radio show?" Otho spins records on WJBB. He reads the soybean and poultry prices and calls up little old ladies on their birthdays and slurps coffee and cracks his cornpone jokes.

"You might better leave that one be," I say. The service bell rings. "Is something up?" I sprint off to the front of the store with Otho following me. He shuffles his big brogan feet like some back alley wino. "Well," he mumbles, "well . . . ."

I'm tallying up the monthly bill for this hog farmer's son while keeping one eye on Otho at the same time. "Spit it out, old boy!" I crow, "what?"

With his face scrunching in on itself, he whispers, "You think I could have that sweet Martin back? At least on the days we're in town . . . ."

The shop door closes behind the hog farmer's son and suddenly the two of us are all alone. Alone with that question still hanging in the air like some loud stink. The shop gone quiet as a library. From down the street a Salvation Army bell chimes the Christmas season on the corner of Lee and Jackson.

"At least on the days we're in town . . ." he repeats, ever so softer. His lower lip quivers slightly as if he's nervous, but I now realize that it always does this. Come to think of it, I've never seen his face not look like this. "If I could just practice, Lon."

His lower lip is still quivering like a playground sissy and I'm getting good and irritated. I'm ill as a damn hornet to be honest. "That don't make sense, O," I blurt out. "You loaned it to me cause I got a knack for it. Remember? You know that. I know that. Hell, everybody knows it." Otho steps back a pace and glances out the store window; his face even pinker now and pinched like biscuit dough. The hog farmer's son is waiting at the curb, hand-rolling a cigarette and glaring across the street at some schoolgirls. "Have you even been listening to how good we sound now? I mean, I got a real knack . . . ."

Otho half-smiles again, in surrender. "All right then," he hisses, and in a ghostlike fashion floats out the door and off down the street and on into the gray day.

That evening I have a nightmare. I am riding backseat of a black town car, slow and steady along a country road in the snow. Long barren fields of white. A bitter wind gusting the drifts around. The car pulls up to stop beside a hunched over fellow wrapped in filthy layers and shivering. It is Otho. I roll the window down to invite him in, but my lips and voice box will not form words. Uh, umm, I say to my old friend. Aaahhr. He is frosted over and blueing of face. He reaches out his crooked right arm to point a long cadaverous index finger at me. Uhhhh. Ohhh. I wake beside Eunice, startled, dry of mouth and shaken.

Your friends are your friends, I realize. Your possessions are meaningless and give the illusion of permanence. I must've read that somewhere and it stuck in somehow among the Crimson Tide football scores and Bible verses. Therefore, I have decided to put in extra hours at the general store to make for a deposit down on a sweet Martin guitar of my own. Otho has been a good friend to me, always. A true friend. I should return the favor, by God, and think of others for a change instead of acting like a damn child all the time. That visit with him and my nightmare have informed me, as Pastor Jimmy would say. I have been informed of what is The Christian Thing To Do.

It's a long haul up to Waterloo, so Dale and I pitch in with Clyde for his driving duties. Otho is beside me but napping while I'm at the wheel. Normally I would say something, as whomever rides shotgun absolutely does *not* nap. They stay awake and alert for the driver with a road map at hand. But that dark dream is still vivid and in front of my mind, so I let it slide and whistle and fidget with the radio instead. Ice pellets are pinging off the windshield and the AM announcer says a winter storm is due tonight.

I want to wake Otho up and tell him my plans. He can take his guitar back after tonight's singing and then I'll drive over to that same shop in Cullman and pick out one this weekend. That will tickle him, I think. It's his sweet Martin, after all. What was I thinking? I glance over, prepared to speak, and see that he's deep in slumber, his mouth wide open, his thin lower lip trembling. The AM station has gone to static and Otho duets with it, lightly snoring. I decide to surprise him later, after the singing.

We end up late to the revival from driving slow on those icy roads. It's a pretty sparse crowd inside the little clapboard church, so the preacher looks relieved to see us and invites us up onstage immediately. Tired and hungry, we stiffly step up, even with ice pellets melting on the shoulders of our coats and in our hair. And we sound tired, and hungry, and cold. Clyde coughs his way through a couple of toe-tappers. Dale drifts in and out of time on the church's out-of-tune piano. Otho can't quite hit those high notes, and I'm not much better with my fingers feeling frostbitten and sluggish upon the strings. But I feel good, not Holy Spirit good, but good nonetheless knowing what I'll tell my old friend after the service. I'd like to see his eyes light up and his lower lip stop trembling.

After the service and the visitation, we're lingering in the main hall surrounded by a few stragglers and their small talk. Clyde is getting that Presbyterian handshake from the preacher — gas and food money for the trip — and I look around and notice that Otho is nowhere to be seen. Dale is chatting with a nice looking middle-aged woman and they're both bundling up in their overcoats. "Dale," says I, "where's Big O?" He glances around and shrugs and returns to his pleasantries. Clyde and the preacher and the stragglers are making their way towards the door. Otho is AWOL.

I'm guessing he's in the bathroom, so I leave the main

hall and head back towards the little choir room where we stowed our gear after the service.

The door is wide open and I stroll in to find Otho standing buck naked in the middle of the room, swaying beneath a bare bulb. His face is fever-red, his manhood aroused. His eyes look crazed and bright and they flare to meet my gaze. It is then that I notice my guitar, *his* guitar, his sweet Martin, shattered in several pieces upon the hardwood floor beneath him.

"Say you got a knack for it, Lon?!" he barks, his face contorted, as twisted and as crooked as his gimpy right arm. "You got a goddamn knack for it?!"

The Second Hurricane

Graying now and tired, Daniel Tanner is, and thus finding himself one Friday night at a Holiday Inn bar in Atlanta. He is attending a music educator's convention. The bar is almost empty, just a few attendees lingering near the exit and two fellows a couple of seats down. The men, Daniel notices with a wistful smile, are holding hands and staring into each other's eyes. Taking this tender scene as a cue, Daniel swigs the last of his beer and stands up to leave. The muted television above the barman flashes a face along with a caption scrolling some breaking news story out of California. Daniel is suddenly frozen. That man, he thinks, I know that man.

The photo on TV displays a face gaunt and bug-eyed, hair close-cropped and a shocking white. The face is staring back at Daniel like some druidic soothsayer. His lips slightly parted as if giving some high-browed musical instruction. Both hands held up in mysterious supplication. The eyes wide open and far seeing. Otherworldly, his expression.

The barman rings up the two men and the place suddenly empties out. Daniel is still standing, jaw dropped, holding his dry pint glass and slowly blinking at the television. It's all coming back to him now. He catches random words from the caption scrawling past: *mass suicide, Hale-Bopp comet, purple cloths, bunk beds*. The barman spies Daniel gawking up at the screen. He grabs the remote and cranks the volume. The man in the photo is, or was rather, a cult leader out West. Along with his female cohort, they taught strict diet and deprivation, meditation and prayer, UFO tracking, male castration. They eventually prescribed strong sedatives and vodka for an appointment with the heavens.

Daniel lowers his head as if in defeat. His eyes go out of focus gazing at the empty pint glass. He hears thunder. The rumble of it rattles the bar windows, and takes him back thirty years or more.

Pale and rail-thin in khakis and a denim shirt, young Daniel sprints in fits and starts, dashing from oak to oak. An unexpected rainstorm is pelting the campus, sending students scurrying about like lab rats electrified. His sweetheart Betsy once said that his loping gait makes him look like a constipated crane unable to lift off in flight. He winces recalling this, and tries evening up his pace. In the crook of his left arm teeters a stack of textbooks. In his right hand a baritone horn in its case. Fall semester is beginning at the state university, and Daniel is soaking wet and late for his first class, Modern Choral Arrangements.

Moving in just the day before, he had unpacked dusty boyhood artifacts and threadbare clothes right in front of his roommate, some dandy named Shelby Wofford. Daniel had shaken hands with this Birmingham boy, perturbed to hear his posh country club accent. The sound of privilege and entitlement, he thinks. The sound of old money and new everything else.

"I do say, but this is cozy, eh?" Shelby smirked. He posed for their cracked room mirror, flexing his thin biceps and flipping his tennis blonde bangs from his forehead. "I'll call father first thing in the morning to straighten out this god-awful mess. You'll see . . . ."

And sure enough, the next morning Daddy Wofford had straightened out the god-awful mess. A phone call to the vice provost had landed young Shelby in his own private room on the ground floor. "No hard feelings, champ," the boy barked on his last trip out of the room. "Best wishes and all that."

Daniel watched as this fop paraded his luggage down the hall. His chest puffed out. His head held high. The world clearly spinning for him and for him alone.

Professor Francis Weeks holds court at the front of the choir room. Small and wiry, his dark hair clipped short, he stands dapper in a dress shirt and slacks a tad too elegant for west central Alabama. The professor's Texas panhandle accent is almost undetectable from years spent living abroad. Like all other incoming music students, Daniel is very much aware of this man's exotic history, his legend, as it were. Those coldwater flats the young Weeks inhabited in gray European cities. The train stations and hostels and corner cafes. Boys and girls as lovers. Each and every one of them lounging after each and every carnal act, smoking hand-rolled hashish cigarettes and sipping red wine. So the story goes, Weeks later returned stateside, wearing his ennui like a Left Bank peacoat. He studied classics and English literature at Sewanee, then voice and piano instruction at Michigan State. He gave away what few possessions he had, stayed enrolled to keep out of Korea, and hopped around from private school to state, teaching during the day and sleeping in cold spartan rooms at night.

Standing atop a wooden riser, Professor Weeks is speaking to the class of habits and intent. His habits. His intent. Those bohemian days long past, he demands of his classes a devotion to choral music that borders on monkish austerity, an intensely focused Zen Buddhist-like lifestyle. Daniel squats in the back row shivering, his clothes dripping, his stomach fluttering from nerves. He pulls out a pencil and opens up a clean notepad. He sits there staring as drops of water fall from his nose and glasses and forehead and make little wet pockmarks upon the blank pages.

"With good and precise habits, with the best of intent" Weeks says, "we can all become as one through our myriad voices. We can use this vessel, Music, to transport ourselves out into celestial wonderment. Even unto the far reaches of heaven itself!"

Daniel's hometown of Pinkard bloats and slumps beside the highway like some roadkill buck dragged off into the weeds. The Tanner family had feuded and farmed and traded and worked mills here since Reconstruction times. Those times were called that, though there was nothing much here to reconstruct. This whole part of the state picked over, then ignored by the crass crows of industry. Subsistence farming. Snake handling churches. Cotton, soybean, pines for clear-cutting. Mythology and ignorance and hatred ripening like melons beneath the summer sun.

The family prodigy, Daniel was, and he shone as a bright light from deep within their dark dank ancestral cave. He astonished onlookers at age five laying tiny fingers upon that old Methodist piano in town. Ma and Pa beaming beside the preacher and his wife. By ten, Daniel was sight-reading hymns, and by junior high he was the church choir accompanist. He even gave the director his two cents worth, when asked, concerning the cantatas for Christmas and for Easter. Handel, the director had joked, was maybe too much for this country bunch to handle.

It's Friday already and still no roommate. Daniel assumes that this is too good to be true. All week, around the corner of each dorm hallway, he half-expects to come upon another snob or (God forbid) a jock heading towards his room lugging their rucksack filled with stink. Maybe Daddy Wofford had inadvertently set him up solo as well, he ponders. By the beginning of week two, the coast seems clear. Three cheers for the House of Wofford! Daniel erupts with a smug tea-sipping accent, posing cheekily before his cracked dresser mirror. He will lay low and avoid parties. He will slink in and out of the cafeteria at odd hours. He will be a hungry ghost singing and haunting the campus, and no one will think to place another student in his room.

The choir is assigned a two-act opera by Aaron Copland, *The Second Hurricane*. Twelve-tone dissonance pokes and prods Daniel's eardrums and reminds him of multiple machines running simultaneously down at the old Pinkard sawmill. Professor Weeks has been impressed by this brassy tenor with obvious perfect pitch, and thus names him sectional leader for the male voices. "Welcome to the lion's den, Daniel," the professor had quipped. Young Tanner accepts the challenge with a quiet pride, and vows to show Weeks that he can rise above his humble hayseed upbringing. He even stays late after class and helps put away sheet music and straightens the chairs and stands. After that initial Biblical joke, the professor remains formal and even a bit distant during their brief interactions. Daniel chalks it up to a brilliant mind being ever focused on the highest of High Art. He has heard rumor that the professor, on occasion, meets students at some undisclosed swimming hole on the Black Warrior River just outside of town. But whatever is showing at the local cinema or on television or who won the big football game last night seems never to be a concern for Francis Weeks. Daniel imagines a vast vault filled with unwritten operas and concertos and symphonies wedged up inside the man's head, all of it tormenting him day and night and waiting to be manifested and unleashed upon our tone-deaf plebeian planet.

Luscious summer weather lingers on into late September. One afternoon as Daniel is walking back from the library, a car honks behind him. He turns in time to see a sky blue convertible jaunting past, Weeks wearing sunglasses behind the wheel and waving in extravagant fashion, grinning. The professor's other arm is draped casually around the boy Shelby, who seems to be sinking down into the passenger seat. The two of them in their undershirts, tanned and river-wet, ride off across campus and into the sunset.

Back in his room, Daniel tries focusing on a music theory assignment, but keeps envisioning Shelby and Weeks embracing in sweaty familiarity. So that's what goes on down at the old swimming hole, he thinks with a mixture of shock, distaste, and more than anything, curiosity. He recalls his prom night with Betsy, and afterwards the way that porch light backlit her long legs as she slowly hiked up her skirt for his hot hand to maneuver through. Now he pictures the professor maneuvering his hot hand upon pale Shelby. Grandmama BoBo said men like that had "sugar in their pockets." He seems to remember her referring to the town florist, Tommy. Daniel now realizes that the world has always spun in this mysterious way, wild, odd and wondrous with all stripes and varieties, and that he's just now opening his eyes to take it all in.

A knock at the door. It's Shelby, still in his undershirt and swim trunks. His face is twisted from its blasé country club mask into something you'd spy in a truckstop mirror, ashen in pallor and downcast. He bites his lower lip and says "Daniel, right?"

Daniel reflexively waves him into the room. Shelby shuffles over and sets his wet-trunked ass down at the end of the bed. Staring at the floor as if just getting a grim doctor's report, he says, "You saw us? Me and Weeks?"

"Saw you?"

From down the hall someone's radio begins blasting a country song. *Please help me I'm falling in love with you . . . .*

Shelby squeezes a leg of his trunks, dribbling water onto the dorm floor. Drip drop. Drip drop. "I told him not to drive us back through campus, the showy old flit." Drip drop. Drip drop.

Daniel suddenly flutters his hands about like bobwhite quail flushed from a field. He blurts out, "I won't tell anyone, Shelby. I promise." He squirms at the sound of his own lie, then adds, "It's really nobody's business, right?" The image just won't leave his mind — Weeks with his dripping arm draped lovingly around the boy. Why had the professor not invited me to swim? Daniel wonders, again feeling a disgusted curiosity. He pictures Weeks, tanned and wet in his swim trunks. Why Shelby? He thinks again. Why someone artless? Someone who undoubtedly makes tone-deaf horrendous vocal noise back home in his family's Episcopal church. Does it all come down to animal lust?

"My daddy will say it *is* his business. That's what he'll say."

An upstairs thud, then muffled laughter. That radio from down the hall even louder now. *Close the door to temptation, don't let me walk through . . . .*

Sitting down on his bed, Daniel can't help but ask, "Was it just the two of you alone at that swimming hole?"

Shelby's eyes have glazed over, maybe for good. "That's what he'll say . . . he'll say it *is* his goddamn business." He stands up abruptly and shuffles towards the door. He looks back at Daniel and whispers, "Please don't tell Daddy about this." His glazed-over eyes water and blink. "Don't tell him I'm this way."

The radio cuts off. "I don't know your daddy, and I barely know you," Daniel replies. "And I can't picture myself having the chance to speak with him." He walks up to Shelby and lowers his voice. "But whatever way you are is beside the point. I just don't think any of us should be off with a teacher...like that, at any rate."

Shelby holds Daniel's gaze for a moment then slowly closes his eyes. A single tear dribbles down his sunburnt cheek. Turning to leave, he whispers once more, "Don't tell him I'm this way."

Slow churn of school weeks — papers, exams, horn exercises. Then cooler weather and leaf scatter. Two weeks until Thanksgiving. The night before the Copland concert, Daniel is in bed just drifting off when he hears voices baying out on the lawn. He creeps across the cold floor and peaks out the window. It's Shelby, who he has not seen since that afternoon with Weeks. He stands beside the open trunk of a luxury sedan weeping, a suitcase in each hand. Who Daniel thinks must surely be Daddy Wofford is throwing boxes into the trunk and yelling at Shelby to buck up. Take it like a man. Stop sniffling and get in the goddamn car.

Daniel slinks back into the warm sheets and feels somewhat sick to his stomach. What have I done? He thinks. Why did I tell? His mind wanders. He sees himself staying late after class to put away sheet music and straighten up the room while Weeks and Shelby frolic together at the swimming hole. Sun-splashed, wet and familiar. He tries picturing Betsy hiking up her skirt after the prom, but cannot. Why did I tell? He thinks again. And just before falling asleep, a thought flashes through Daniel's mind — Weeks saw me seeing them. Weeks with his fancy sunglasses. His wet hair, his tan smirk. Daniel realizes that Weeks knows that he knows.

The choir meets at 6pm, dressed formally, for warm-ups. No Weeks. Half and hour until show time and still no Weeks. At 6:45, a quiet mutiny is brewing amongst the tenors and sopranos. No Weeks, no concert, they whine. A sadly plump baritone from Sylacauga, name of Chauncy, stands his ground. He points at Daniel and screeches, "We've got *him*, haven't we?"

Everyone in the rehearsal room turns and looks Daniel's way. He sees it all in their faces. Fear, hurt, anger, apathy. He himself feels a little bit of each, and yet somehow summons the courage to shout out, "By all that shits, let us put on this concert!"

The audience sits enthralled from the very first note. Daniel's sight reading prowess has him at an advantage over the typical student, but this Copland opera is difficult, nuanced. Cursing under his breath and sweating, he directs it all on the fly. The choir, being suddenly liberated from professorial oversight, relaxes and collectively leans into each measure, each phrase. Near the end, it hits Daniel like an epiphany. This musical work concerns a group of young people stranded by a hurricane. They all have to work together for the greater good. They all have to take ownership of their own circumstances, and rely upon each other just to survive.

Next morning, the news of Weeks' termination spreads quickly across campus. He had been confronted hours before the concert concerning his relations to the male student (to which he confirmed), and then promptly told to leave campus. The Wofford boy was, at the very least, "of age," but community standards still deemed it a horrendous depravity. And since the state university historically overlooks its music department and its doings, the professor's obligation for that evening was not even known about to bring up for discussion.

Daniel can only imagine Daddy Wofford being beside himself in his Vestavia Hills mock Tudor mansion. Pulling all his financial support. Drawing up legal papers and such. Oh the pious rage he will most certainly direct at that professor, and yet a blind eye (willful?) to be cast towards his own heartbroken son. He can just hear Wofford roaring, "How dare that perverted shit! What sort of California fairyland produces these defects?" And sweet Shelby all alone, fading away in his upstairs loft. Surely he is staring teary-eyed out the window like some captive maiden in yon medieval times.

The Copland concert gives Daniel quite an ego boost. His classmates in choir teasingly refer to him as "Maestro," and he now feels brave and secure enough to laugh along with them. The semester finishes in a blur of sheet music, horn recitals, and typed essays submitted to the teaching assistant. The essays just busy work, really, as each student receives an automatic passing grade for the class. The scandal is all but forgotten in the rush up to finals, and it's not until Christmas break back in Pinkard that Daniel begins to process it. His role in it. Surely he wasn't the only student who knew, or said anything. There they were parading their affections about, after all, in broad daylight and right through the middle of campus. He and his mother sit and sip coffee in the afternoons, glancing out the window at her bird feeders buzzing with finches, but really Daniel is just visualizing Shelby's dreary face floating before him. They sit and sip coffee, he and his mother. A ham or a turkey thawing in the kitchen sink, the faucet drip-dropping. Daniel sees Shelby squeezing out his swim trunks. Drip drop. Drip drop.

And what happens next is simply life passing at its various speeds. Daniel graduates with honors and moves back to Pinkard to be near mother and daddy. The home hearth burning. The old Main Street slow and graveyard quiet late of evenings. No mystery to solve. No drama to endure. That church choir awaited him, and so he succumbs to it all — the wisteria-scented small town heaviness, the torpor of his daydreams, such pointless existence, ad nauseum. And what is time, exactly? He considers. Or love, for that matter. He marries his high school sweetheart Betsy, who also waited, and they begat two dull Pinkard children who in turn grow (again, various speeds) dove-plump and fledge, landing just a few miles away to roost and rear their own dull offspring. The university and the choir and the river all slowly fade away. The blur of youth. The mixed-up knee-jerk emotions. His jealousy of Shelby over the attention from Weeks. That sycophantic tattletale prude he became. All fading. His days click-clack by like that sound the old Norfolk Southern makes rumbling its way out of town.

Another clap of Georgia thunder brings Daniel back to the Holiday Inn. The weather further away now and moving off to the east. A truck commercial on the bar TV is blasting heavy metal music with a WWF announcer's voice. Hey Atlanta! Buy now with no money down! Daniel shakes his head as if clearing his ears of swimming pool water. Professor Weeks is the man on TV. He has led a group of young people to their pathetic and unnecessary deaths. Their sad stupid little Nikes poking out from beneath purple cloths.

He glances down the bar to find the place completely empty, then hears a clunk coming from an open door past the television. The barman is back there stacking cases of beer for the coming weekend. Daniel wants to tell the man everything. He wants to tell him about Pinkard and the state university, about Shelby and Weeks. He wants to tell him that he was the one who spoke up, but now cannot recall why he did such a thing. He wants to tell the barman about Betsy and their kids, about the way that one Main Street red-light changes colors slower than any other one he's ever sat at. He wants to tell him how his incredibly uneventful life has flashed past him like some sort of astrological debris. Instead, he lays a twenty beside his pint glass and steps outside into a vacant parking lot for some fresh air.

It's much later than he would typically stay up. He needs to get back to his room to go over notes for tomorrow morning's panel on twentieth century American avant-garde music. With a smile, he recalls the Copland work. How they all pulled together at a time of great shock and sadness to make such joyful noise unto the Lord. The night air is brisk. The rain has stopped. The sky above him and to the west clear. Daniel stares up into the vast darkness with a longing to see something amazing, something large and meaningful. He then realizes that the city lights are too bright, too strong, and that whatever it is hovering up there was never meant to be seen by him anyway.

Me and the Devil
Blues

Brother Cecil tunes up his mandolin backstage of the union hall. He makes chicken scratch sounds plucking it, a lit cigarillo dangling from his thin lips. Its smoke wafts about the small room like some thurifer's church incense. He tunes and plucks some more. "How's it look out there?"

A crowd has gathered other side of the stage curtain. Low murmuring. A cough or a cackle every now and then. Local folk. A mix. Townspeople and cotton farmers and roughnecks and miners. Teenagers, some of them. A little undercurrent of electricity in the air. Anticipation. Radio play tends to put asses in chairs, I've found.

"Go look for yourself," I say. "I don't aim to peek."

"You ain't nervous are you, big brother?"

"Shitfire."

"Shit fire and we'll all be warm."

A stagehand leans around the corner and says "Five minutes to show, boys." Cecil says all right and stubs out his cigarillo and starts wailing on the mandolin. Really stroking the neck, like he's working on a heifer's tit. I grab my Martin guitar from the couch and picture grandmommy milking her cow every morning during the summers we stayed with her. She'd say, "Come on you old bitch," and start squeezing. She'd half-fill a bucket with the steaming froth, then call me and my brother over closer and point the teat at us and squirt us good. We would both squeal and run off and hear her laughing and laughing.

"Let's do this thing, cowboy," Cecil says. "I hear them greenback dollars calling my name!"

The crowd goes quiet and the curtains twitch a bit. "Ladies and gentlemen. You've heard them on WJBB. Now get ready for the real deal. All the way from Delmar, Alabama . . . please welcome the Jasper Brothers! Cecil and Ray!"

Raucous applause and blinding stage lights. That stagehand just brushing past us as Cecil is already strumming the intro to *Birmingham Boogie Woogie*, our opener. He seems set aflame by the crowd's electricity. His whole body bigger, taller, his eyes dark and bright at the same time. That crazed smile of his flashing jagged wolf teeth. I hold on for dear life and start strumming my goddamn G chord.

We run our set and the crowd stays with us the whole way. Hoots and hollers and laughter at my knock-knock jokes. *Mountain Dew, Dust On The Bible*. Cecil pushes the tempo on each song like he's sprinting for the endzone on a fourth down call. I have to stomp time with my brogan on that creaky clapboard stage periodically to pull us back to a sensible pace. Cecil's sweet strings trilling like some springtime birdsong, his high lonesome holler hanging up in the rafters long after the final chord fades.

I stuff the evening's take into my duffel bag after counting it twice. Not bad for the boonies. Not bad considering I could be back at our uncle's mill busting my backside. I pack up my Martin and grab the duffel bag and give the little backstage room a second glance before heading out to the car.

Cecil is chatting up a pretty thing by the curb. She giggles and twirls her dark curls and playfully slaps his hand every now and then. His mandolin lays eschew on top of our Ford. A thick fog rolling in from that reservoir south of town. "Let's hit the road C," I say, maybe a little too sharply. The girl giggles once more and hands Cecil a folded slip of paper, which he slips inside his suit coat pocket, grinning all the while like a damn Cheshire cat. "You got it, big brother," he sings in a vaudeville manner. The girl laughs so hard she snorts.

Our days and weeks drag by like the backend coal carts of a Memphis-bound Southern Pacific. Drive, play, sleep. Drive, play, sleep. Except Cecil tends to leave that last one off, especially when there's a pretty thing waiting at the curb. And there usually is — for him. The shows pay out decent enough and radio play is still good. And we pack these little halls farther north than either of us would have ever imagined. Cincinnati, Evansville, Moline, Ft. Wayne. Any sizable place with a mill or a factory filled with transplanted hillbilly workers who own a radio. Good folk who just want to hear music that reminds them of home, I guess. But like I said: drive, play, sleep. That will wear down a soul after awhile.

And speaking of souls, Cecil brings his up unexpectedly in conversation late one afternoon over black coffee at a roadside diner outside of Jackson, Tennessee. "Brother," he says, "are you still a believer? Sin? Eternity? All that?" I sip and set my mug down and stare out the window at a tractor-trailer filled with cotton rumbling by, headed north. Sunset the color of a bruised peach. I clear my throat a time or two.

"I try to believe, C," I say, "I really do. But it's getting damn hard the further I get down the road." I turn my coffee mug so that the handle is perpendicular to the table's edge. "Why do you ask?"

"Just chewing on it of late. A lot of time to think out here, rambling." He picks his fork through a plate of scrambled eggs while staring at the side of a napkin dispenser. Like he's looking into a crystal ball. Like he's spying his funhouse mirror face blown up into some sad-assed balloon. "It's as if the Holy Spirit didn't stick with me, I reckon."

"You don't know that. I don't know that. Nobody really knows anything but . . . ."

"Ray, I get off stage some nights and feel a tiny hellfire burning in my gut. I look at these backstage gals and just want to eat them alive. I can still smell and taste them sitting right here talking to you. I want them all to bow down before me and offer up their bodies as sacrifice. I want to defile one after the other and then move on to the next town! I want . . . ."

"Hey now brother, keep it down." Folks at nearby tables are either sideways glancing at us or flat out gawking. The waitress brings our check and without looking at it I drop some wrinkled greasy bills on the table and we duck out quickly.

The very next day our show at the Senatobia, Mississippi freemason hall goes off like a wet fart. I feel a sore throat and aches coming on, so there's that. But Cecil and his manic demonic drive? Cecil and his furious fingers flying over the fretboard? Cecil with his country boy hard-on and his tongue wagging at all that high school snatch?

He stands there beside me off to the left of the microphone like a cigar store Indian, weakly riffing and mumbling through his harmony lines. I stare him down after the second song but he won't make eye contact. With me or the crowd. There's polite applause the rest of the way, but no encore called for. Folks can usually sense a train wreck coming. By the time I get to our car with my Martin and the evening's take, Cecil's in the back seat smoking with all the windows rolled down. A half-finished pint bottle wedged in his lap. His mandolin laying on the front passenger seat like an abandoned baby.

"Let's roll, daddy-O," he sings.

We both decide to splurge and get some decent rest for a day or so before our next show in Belzoni. But after I shower and climb into bed, Cecil, grinning that crazy wolf grin, says, "I'll be back shortly." Then he grabs the car keys and slips out the door. *To hell with you,* I think, and roll over and drift into a dead man's slumber.

I'm startled awake well after midnight by Cecil barging into our motor court cottage. He has a glow around his whole body and seems to be levitating in the center of the room. "Ray," he whispers in what sounds like an old woman's rasp, "Ray, I gone and done it. Hell yes I did . . . ."

I'm still half-asleep and blurry-eyed, but that voice of his brings chill bumps to my bare arms. "Brother," I say, "where you been?" His glowing form hovering in the center of the room. Soft night sounds from out on the highway. "Where you been, boy?" He starts giggling like a little girl and those chill bumps on my arms start spreading all over.

"I done it, Ray, I done it! The crossroads like they say." Cecil's face suddenly blank. Chalky white. His eyes two little red dots like lit cigarette ends. He licks his corpse-pale lips and continues. "That girl up in Greenwood? Janelle? Janelle said . . . ."

"C! Another damned colored girl? Christ! Hasn't she and her people suffered enough already without having to deal with your skinny white ass? What would daddy think about this? Hell, what would *her* daddy think about this?"

"I don't give two shits, Ray! Daddy is just dust and bones in a pine box! He added up to nothing . . . like everybody else! But not me, goddamnit. Not me . . . ."

My brother's bright glow has faded a touch. His eyes closer to gray-blue, his voice sounding suddenly weak. Beaten. He takes a seat by the window and leans forward, cupping his hands like he's about to tell me my childhood coon dog has died again.

"Yeah I spent that night with Janelle. Don't give a shit what y'all think." He scratches at a gauzy bandage I've just now noticed. It's on his left wrist with a rust-colored circle in the center of it. "She told me about where Highway 12 meets 49 up near Tchula . . . she said to go there at midnight with my blood in a pint bottle."

You son of a bitch, I think, as my brain-to-mouth connection has stopped working. I continue staring at him, slack-jawed and still not quite sure that I'm awake.

"It's for real, cowboy," Cecil whispers. "For real . . . ."

Over the next hour or so, I hear tale about a driverless black limousine appearing before my brother out on Highway 49 at midnight. Driverless. Noiseless. A mirrored back window rolling down and a cold skeletal hand reaching out to take the bottle of blood. Driverless.

Noiseless. Cecil standing there on the side of the road feeling lightheaded and weak-kneed. Cecil wanting the Holy Spirit to come into his life, but choosing the wrong one. The Unholy Spirit. Driverless. Noiseless. The car pulling away, headed north towards Clarksdale or Memphis or wherever the hell Lucifer wants to go.

"I can't figure out why, C? Why do this?" I've crawled back into bed now, my legs aching and my throat still sore, but with a feeling that sleep isn't coming anytime soon.

"So you believe me, then?"

"Shit no, I don't believe you!" I kick weakly at the threadbare sheets tucked too tightly under the bed corners. "You don't hardly sleep or eat and you drink like a damn Paddy. It's a wonder that some Satanic vision hasn't hopped up on stage with us yet."

"I just wanted what all those others got," he says, grinning and baring his wolf teeth, "and now I have it. I know I have it."

I stare at him for a full minute without responding. Without blinking.

"Tommy Johnson!" He blurts out. "Robert . . . ."

"I know their damn names, Cecil! But what does all that have to do with you? With us, you fool?"

My brother lowers his face and turns slowly away from me. His shoulders are slumped as he drags ass out the door, shutting it quietly behind him as if he's trying not to disturb my sleep. As if he hasn't already disturbed my sleep for tonight, and pretty much every night since.

The crowd in Belzoni is bucking and snorting and stamping their feet well before showtime. A buzzing in the ears. Crackling in the air. The Confederate-era town hall is shaking, and seems to sway and reverberate with small town manic enthusiasm.

Cecil has a smoky tang hovering about his body, but his eyes have gone coal-black and lifeless. We haven't spoken to each other since the night before in the motor lodge, or early this morning, rather. He looks as if he's been poured into his easy chair in a dark corner of our backstage room. His hands pale and still in his lap. His mandolin tossed and forgotten upon the ratty couch.

"Let's do it, partner," I say, strapping on my Martin and buttoning up my suit coat. "Let's give Belzoni a little bit of *you know what.*"

Cecil looks up at me, slowly blinking. "You know what?"

"It's just a figure of speech, C," I say. "Come on! Let's get on with it, br . . . ."

"You mean *hell*, right?"

I watch as my brother rises from his chair and floats over to the couch to grab his mandolin. He holds it at his side like an axe or a cudgel as he floats past me and out of the room and towards the side-stage. I shake my head a time or two. I rub my eyes. In the cracked mirror before me, I see a paunchy and sad-looking fellow on the cusp of middle age. His face gone gaunt and stricken. His daddy's guitar hanging limp at his side.

Quiet as the grave, this Belzoni crowd. All buzz and electricity dissipated from the air. All sense of right or wrong stomped down into the piney floor. I step out on the stage, waving to the yokels in my good pressed suit, but their eyes are fixed upon Cecil. He is levitating demonically behind his microphone.

Like nothing out of the ordinary is happening, I take

a deep breath and fill my lungs with the smoky sulfurous tang around me. I start counting us in for our opening boogie woogie, bracing for my big G chord. Just then Cecil's feet burst into flames and he begins howling like a damn werewolf. Within seconds his whole body is engulfed in a hell-hot fire as the crowd screams and scatters into the night. I stumble backwards away from the burning miasma, my Martin strings popping off one by one in the heat. The hall completely emptied out. I drop to my knees like a sinner at Golgotha and look upon my brother's ashes drifting about the stage.

Dwayne from Texas

The beach I'm always standing on is from my childhood. There's a bitter wind blowing off that choppy Gulf water, cold as hell. Nova Scotia or New England cold. Then I turn around and there's this ridiculous, gargantuan bonfire. A city block long and two shitting stories high. I guess that's technically not a bonfire but a wildfire. But the moment I see it, I just know it's a bonfire. Only there's absolutely no heat coming off of it. None. Like it's just a giant hologram or something I'm watching on an NFL jumbotron. And then my high school marching band thunders by, blasting for all they're worth but the volume is muted. The only sound is the crackling of the heatless fire. Flag girls and majorettes jiggle by, completely nude and all winking at me. Muted brass, snare. Little Tommy Winston's all red-faced, smooching his tuba. The bonfire snapping, popping. At the procession's end, a clopping burro pulls this old pine box labeled: HOFFMAN, DWAYNE WAYNE. CLASS OF 1987. VOTED LEAST LIKELY TO MATTER.

Burning one down with some cold coffee, I take stock of my body odor, now mixed with an oily, herbal stench. It's not all that bad, considering our apartment's one washing machine has been out of order for several weeks and all my complaints to the tiny Latino landlord fall on tiny deaf ears. Little golden-brown empanada ears. And eventually I begin to realize the hypocrisy of my complaining, as it was I who had ravaged and befouled the machine in the first place. A couple of bottles of cheap wine with my friend Sumter turned into a 4 a.m. dry-humping contest involving said washing machine. He and I on either side, pumping away. With my friend being the more seasoned and suave lover, I finished first. I won, or lost rather. We probably jarred something loose in the whole electrical outlet water-pipe grounding-wire thingamajig. So I stopped complaining to Mendoza.

And the nearest shitting Laundromat is a half-hour schlep away because the 37 bus doesn't go on that route. Come to think of it, the 37 bus is the exact source of my stink. It is a *pissoir* on wheels, a metal tube full of strange and magnificent low-income odors. It provides the smell foundation upon which my own bacteria build their little refuges of reek. On top of that, I have to squeeze in between the fat rolls of women smacking gum and reading those evil red Harlequin romance paperbacks. Christ, I hate those things.

The thing is, though, I have to go to work. Today's my first day and I've got to clean my act up. Hired by the Boys and Girls Club. Are you kidding? I'll try almost anything once. On my application under the question *What is the most important thing you possess to offer the children of today?* I simply wrote: *My two hands to choke them with, if necessary.* And I'm thinking there's no way they could've possibly deciphered my handwriting; otherwise I would not be searching my shithole of an apartment for clean work clothes.

They say the first day on the job is the most important, but I disagree. Hell, they've already hired you. They desperately want you to work out; otherwise they're short-staffed and interviewing again. I've yet to test it, but I have a theory that one could show up the first day to almost any job completely nude, screaming on peyote, and most managers would overlook it as just a bad case of nerves. My next gig, I'll check that out.

I'll be damned, look at that. Back of the closet, a clean navy blue polo shirt. Now if only I could find my newish khakis. Not those other ones, stained by laundry love.

A humongous black man greets me in the Boys and Girls Club parking lot. He is outfitted in baggy designer jeans, Terminator-style muscles stretching his tight gray t-shirt. With a steady gaze into my own bloodshot eyes, he inquires in a thick French-Creole accent, "Are you Dwayne Hoffman?"

"Yessir."

"Benoit Didot," he says. "Nice to meet you, sir."

My god that's a suave fucking accent. Brother must get all the ladies talking like that. Jesus Christ! DO NOT call him *brother*. DO NOT even think the word *brother*, you Jerry Springer show racist hick. Easy, man. Calm your ass down...

"It's nice to meet you too, sir," I reply. OK, that's better. Nice and easy, sleazy.

So, the workday passes smoothly, and Benoit is actually pretty cool. He's lived in Texas for several years and likes it all right. Most anything's better than Ghana, he says. He's almost finished with grad school in early childhood development at the university. We each crack a few jokes about life here in River City. Dumbass frat guys, loser musicians, New Age crystal lickers, jarhead Baptist state senators. Now *that's* a place to set up shop!

Did I say 'the workday passes smoothly?' What I meant was – 'before the shitting children arrived, all sugar-shocked from their after-school vending machine goo . . . the workday blahblahblah.' What a goddamn nightmare! These four-feet-tall, two-hundred-pound monsters! These catch-phrase-spouting, video-game-tweaking trolls! All cursing and belching and laughing and farting and MTV-dancing and gum-smacking uselessness.

Oh for the Family Planning Policy of the People's Republic, I think. Oh for a devastating return of the Bubonic Plague! I look around the room for Benoit and see him jangling his car keys, ducking quickly out the back door.

See Sumter standing there, astride the jukebox, a damn good friend. He of the clean, pressed blue jeans, the short-sleeved leisure shirt, tucked in. Always tucked in. He of the tan loafers and shiny, balding pate. He of the prodigious gut, all full of pinto beans and smoked brisket and cold Mexican beer. He who presses that belly up against the music machine, his out-y button selecting songs of its own. Zeppelin, Sabbath, Jim Croce.

Sumter Spivey of the South Texas Spiveys. Big ranching family west of Corpus Christi. The Body of Christ, he calls it. Going home to visit daddy and take him to communion at The Body of Christ, he says. Which means he and his daddy shooting tequila, knee-walking from one cantina to the next, hurling up their enchilada dinners along the way.

When Sumter's granddaddy got killed in Korea, Daddy Spivey took over the family spread and tore down the old cedar post sign that read Spivey Ranch. He handcrafted a new one from old found bits of rusted metal and whatnot. Crafted it into a monstrosity of a road sign that read TURD BLOSSOM RANCH, NO GODDAMN TRESPASSING. Church folk called it in not long after he hung it up. Daddy got a visit from two Nueces County officials the very next day. He brought out some cold Modelos, salt-rimmed and with lime slices. The three of them had a good laugh. Drive friendly, said Daddy as the officers lurched their cruiser out onto the highway. Both grinning, pinkfaced and sweaty.

Nat King Cole's *The Christmas Song* starts chiming over the bar's speaker system. Sumter turns back to me, his right hand flashing devil horns, his stubby, discolored tongue wagging *a la* Gene Simmons.

"I can't take this fucking heat, Hoff," he yells. "Shitting one hundred and five degrees today. I can't take it anymore. Holiday classics for me tonight."

He had asked me to join him here, a skid mark of a place called BoBo's. At least it's dark and the jukebox is varied and when Sumter's co-worker shows up with a bag of Bastrop County psilocybin mushrooms (and some extra, for Sumter to sale), we won't feel so conspicuous. But then Sumter's already half-lit, fa-la-la-ing in falsetto. He's loaded twenty dollars worth of quarters on Christmas carols. So much for the stealthy pickup.

A swarthy man hulking over in the exit corner and resembling some Lou Ferrigno / Boris Yeltsin lab-created love child gives my friend the stink eye as he lopes back towards the bar. "It's not even June yet, brother," I offer. "And you're basically from Ol' Mexico. What are you complaining about?"

Sumter retrieves his vodka tonic and swirls it a moment,

visibly enjoying the splinky sounds of ice cubes. "Remember two years ago, I spent the summer in Denver with Caroline?" I grimace and take a quick pull on my Lone Star. The muted TV above the bar is showing a commercial for abused puppies and kittens and a number you can call to send in money to help stop such a thing. Then a hot middle-aged hippy lady appears on the screen, talking up this endeavor. Luckily, as I said, the TV is muted. What a ridiculous shitting world, I'm thinking, and Sumter says, "Hey asshole, I'm talking here. I spent that summer in the Rockies . . . "

"Sorry, sorry," I mumble. "Right . . . the Rockies. Nice and cool, huh?"

Sumter stares me down for a few seconds. "Yes, bitch. Nice and cool up there. I do believe, however, that it reset my biological thermostat. And now, Texas heat is killing me. Just walking from Sissy's backyard, which is shaded by the way, to my car on the street, is sheer torture. Against the Geneva Convention type shit, my man." His Aunt Sissy, Sissy Spivey of the South Texas Spiveys, lets her nephew crash in the makeshift toolshed/apartment squatting unceremoniously beneath her two dying pecan trees. He cleans her house once a week, cooks dinner, shares weed. Everything a widowed, swinging aunt could desire in a nephew.

Christmas in Dixie by Alabama queues up next. The Incredible Yeltsin Hulk over by the exit corner moans out loud "For Christ's sake!" He glares at Sumter and myself. We both send kissy baby suck faces his way, then slowly turn back to our drinks.

"Biological thermostat? The fuck are you all of sudden, that wheelchair science dude?"

Christmas in Dixie, it's snowing in the pines! Sumter sings out loud, drawing another stink eye from Yeltsin Hulk. *Merry Christmas from Dixie to everyone tonight* . . . "Christ! he screams. "Did this singer's four-year-old mongoloid child write these lyrics?"

"Amigo, keep it down," I say. "Let's chill it a bit. Look . . . our drinky-poos."

Sumter sips his and then sighs, "I wonder what Santa's bringing me this year . . . ."

"Have you seen that commercial with the dying puppies?" I ask. Changing the subject with Sumter is always the conversation's highest priority. "That's what's wrong with this stupid country . . . ."

"Oh shit! Here we go . . . ."

"We treat our pets like people and our people like animals. Folks starving all over the goddamn world, but only the best for Lil' Brownie! Fucking free-range fair trade organic kibbles, brother! That's another thing . . . ."

And from Fort Payne Alabama . . . .*Take care now, God bless y'all* . . . Sumter has climbed up onto the bar and he's rubbing his crotch while crooning. *Merry Christmas, to – night!*

Within seconds, Yeltsin Hulk was on us both and then all was painted black.

Dwayne do this. Dwayne do that. Don't track mud in the house, Dwayne, momma just vacuumed. Boy, where's that damn beer I asked you for five minutes ago? Take them muddy shoes off outside, Dwayne. I told you not to play outside today. It's a damn tropical storm out there. Almost to Galveston, they say. You some kind of retard, boy? A beer, goddamnit. Bee-yer! Dwayne, have you finished your homework, honey? You like them math problems, don't you? Hell, boy, this beer ain't even cold. Get one from the back of the fridge. Don't give me that look boy.

I know I ain't your real daddy but I sure as shit will give you the ass-whooping of your life if you look at me like that again. Dwayne honey, the trash needs taking out and Jimmy's asleep already. He works so hard for us down at the plant, honey. Just take it out and then you can finish your TV show. You did your math problems, Dwayne? Honey, momma can't pick you up after school tomorrow, I've got an interview out at the new airport. I put some bus money on your dresser. Boy, turn that damn TV off and get your ass in bed. You hear me boy?

I never saw Benoit Didot again. Bastard had escorted me through the front door and then hauled his ass out the back. If I knew enough about this Boys and Girls Club organization, I'd report him to headquarters, wherever the hell that is. Haven't even seen the telephone. The kids and I have just been sitting around the rec room after school, eating potato chips I bought in bulk and watching old WWF videotapes.

And as you can guess, that First Day On the Job Magic Mushroom Celebration with Sumter didn't pan out as planned. Why exactly had he chosen a crowded bar to make a transaction for Class C hallucinogenics? I've stopped asking these types of questions concerning him. Turns out Yeltsin was the one holding Sumter's order, not the coworker. His ass got carted off to downtown booking, with prior offenses, one could imagine. Caroline, Sumter's off-and-on girl, had set up the deal all the way from Denver, thinking that Sumter had already met and partied with this Hulk. I had not, but it's possible Sumter might've come across the guy during some pagan evening in his past. Mister Short-Term Memory, we call him from time to time, while singing that stupid *Saturday Night Live* skit song.

The bar owner had taken pity on us, being regulars and all, and covered for us when the police arrived. No sir, these gentlemen were not causing a public disturbance, and no, that gentleman there did not expose himself while singing Christmas carols. No sir, I don't care what them folks over there say. Just sitting here having a respectable drink, they was. Then this madman attacks them. Out of nowhere.

Sumter bore the brunt of it. Went to the emergency room with a busted jaw, black eyes, and a broken left pinky. I'll never play the piano again, he had screamed. I, on the other hand, sustained a puffy lower lip from Yeltsin's stray elbow and a nasty thigh bruise from slipping in spilled booze and playing dead on the bar floor. But other than that, I was fine. Momma didn't raise no fool.

After the drama wound down, I paid our tab and hit the men's room. To the left of the lone commode, in the unmistakable scrawl of my friend, was displayed a limerick:

Here I stand, all sweaty-pitted
Tried to fart, but must've shitted

Right after the hospital visit, Sumter hightails it back to South Texas, to the ranch. He figures on laying low for a while. Cutting brush, feeding chickens, picking peppers. Country shit, he calls it. He tells Sissy he will be away for several weeks and that Daddy Spivey, being ill, needs help, what with Jorge the Gardener visiting family down in San Luis Potosi.

The fat little boy stays later than everyone else. He always sports the same sweaty oversized San Antonio Spurs t-shirt and a smattering of Cheetos dust around his lips. I'm trying to straighten up everything and close up shop, but he just stands there by the bookshelf like some pudgy garden gnome, holding a tattered copy of *Goodnight, Moon*, pleading with his tiny and sad almond eyes for me to read to him.

"Angel, I don't have time to do that today," I snap.

"It's *An-hel*," he replies, still holding up the book with his right hand, now scratching his ass with the left.

"That's great," I say. "I'll remember that. Now do me favor and vamanos. Your mami should be here any moment. Go outside and play in the street or something . . . ."

He keeps standing there holding up the book, scratching his ass, staring at me with those vacant, sadly beautiful almond eyes.

See Daddy Spivey, horizontal now and lips sewn shut. He of the beerbelly bloating out from beneath his too-small Longhorn t-shirt. Pit-stained from brisket sweat. He of the sunburned leather face, heavily powdered now for meeting up with Jesus. Who the hell would want an open-casket outdoors funeral under a south Texas sun? Daddy Spivey, that's who.

"Jorge would've loved this," speaks Sumter to the smallish crowd, all drip-browed and squinting. "The complete audacity to lie dead and rotting beneath our very idea of heaven. This Chinese-made athletic t-shirt barely stretching over his pale and bluish stomach. Mariachi music, beef fajita tacos. What's left of the family, arguing over heirlooms, making a shitting mess of the yard, the kitchen. And God above, whom we all created, not listening, not listening . . . Yes, Jorge would've loved this, but alas, he's with his *familia*, down south. As for Daddy, he would've told you all to get off his property and go fuck yourselves . . . Amen."

"Amen" echoes the sunburnt mix of nephews and cousins and half-sisters, all of them refilling their plastic cups from a live oak-shaded keg, darting their eyes back and forth over the outdoor hacienda furniture and the Mission style pottery and the fine sculptures.

Angel keeps asking me where LeBron is. He's staying late again and I'm dying for a drink and a smoke. His mother works three jobs, I've since found out. LeBron? he asks.

I've guessed that he's talking about Benoit. We've just finished another run through *Goodnight Moon*, and Angel is tugging at his Spurs t-shirt, looking restless. "LeBron is on TV, Angel." I say. "He's famous. NBA and all that. You're thinking of the guy that used to work here? Benoit?"

The boy's face looks like a bowl of tapioca pudding. His mouth slightly parted and drooling. "Ben-Wah," I growl in a Darth Vader voice. "Bennn-Waaah". Angel starts giggling and scratching his ass.

The 37 bus has topped itself today. Dregs of humanity. Us at our worst. The odor has gone beyond the cologne of midsummer funk and straight into an *Eau de* Early Autumn Bucket Full of Pus and Bile. There's a crazy bastard holding court up beside the driver. Child-sized, hunchbacked in a thriftstore flannel shirt, he has taped-up Buddy Holly glasses and grips a paperback copy of *Das Kapital* like it's the Bible. His other hand waves wildly at the driver, an index finger inflecting upwards with each point made.

The phone rings and it's Sumter, tequila-slurring his words, strange scrubland birds calling in the background. It's been a month or so since the funeral and he sounds lighter, less put-upon by the duties of existence. I'm laying on my couch listening to *Mule Variations*, the Tom Waits CD I stole last week from the local library, ice cracking in a tumbler of Jack on my coffee table. Those Boys and Girls Club kids were especially manic this afternoon. Legs and feet and lower back sore from all that standing and crouching and my head is pounding from what I'm afraid is not just a headache, but also me starting to give a damn.

"Sorry I couldn't make it down there, amigo," I say. "My job and all."

A slight pause, his exhaling of smoke, then "Yeah yeah . . . no worries, Hoff. He didn't notice . . . but check it out, Caroline showed up. She's taken me back, man. Taken me back . . . yeah."

"That's great, fella. I mean, if that's what you want."

Another pause, more exhaling, "Of course it's what I want, you shit. You know that. Anyway, when I get everything settled down here, I'm moving up to Denver. She's planning this huge Labor Day bash with a friend. They've got this massive backyard surrounded by deaf old neighbors who can't hear it thunder. Live music, light show, illicit ladies and sweet substances. You've got to come up, Hoff, for real."

I picture another hopelessly doomed road trip with Sumter. Never the interstate, only back roads. Deer jerky and warm cans of Lone Star. Peeing in empty milk jugs. Endless loops of FM country and classic rock. No stopping, ever, except for flat tires, overheated engines. The always very-possible DUI. Panhandle jails.

"Man that sounds like a hoot . . . but I can't take any time off."

"Can't, or won't?"

"Oh come on," I sputter, "I'm really trying here. Plus, there's this little boy . . . . "

"Holy Christ, Hoff, not a little boy!"

"You shitting pervert!" I shout, turning down Waits. "It's not that. He's just this tubby little kid named Angel. *An-hel*, rather. His mom is late most days and I've been reading to him. *Goodnight, Moon* and shit like that. He's a sad little bastard, Sumter . . . . ."

One last pause, no exhaling, "That's wonderful, Hoff...seriously. I'll call you when I settle in up there. Take care, brother."

See Dwayne Hoffman. Dwayne from Texas. Strolling through the night surf, that Gulf still choppy, that wind cutting and cold. The humongous bonfire has been replaced by a Pink Floyd laser light show. Twenty yards or so up the beach stands Sumter in a Rocky Mountain parka. He's fiddling with knobs inside some freestanding metallic closet-like contraption. Pay no attention to this man inside your dreams, Hoff, he barks. Multicolored laser beams pulse and strobe upon the low Gulf clouds. No music, no sounds of surf or wind. Just the soft clopping of that burro in the khaki-colored sand. On it rides little Angel and his mother. She's hugging him close like he's a teddy bear or a pillow. He's reading to her from his book, pointing out the pictures. They draw near, look up and wave, then pass by, bobbing up and down with the burro's slow, steady gait.

The Body is a Temple

That harelipped Claunch boy always did play too close to the highway. Snotty towheaded shit-ass of a child. His mama all but filling up their sofa with her junk food heifer girth. Watching her stories all day. His daddy Joe down at the textile mill or corn-drunk with his buddies out at the lake. Those older ones at school but there he was running wild at all hours. Side of the highway throwing dirt clods. Hollering cuss words. Pulling out his tiny child pecker to point at passing cars.

I'll just say that my own boy, Tommy, wasn't much better. Yet Martha, my dear departed, kept him in line somehow. I sure as hell didn't help. Lovely Lloyd they called me, and still call me for going on seventy damned years in this bad job of a town. I owned and operated Lovely Lloyd's Filling Station on Highway 43. A sad cinder block hovel squatting by the side of the road like a mama cat about to drop her litter. Folks gassed up here and bought sundries and Co-Colas and hard candy and basically just shot the shit with me. I closed her up back when Martha passed and now I just sit here on my ass and watch traffic pass bound for Tupelo or Birmingham.

Heading home from town just now in a hurry and this

radio preacher comes on and says that "the body is a temple" and all that, which I've heard before and still don't quite understand or believe. I'm still pondering this when the front of my Buick explodes like a damn watermelon all over the place. I squeal to a stop and cut the radio off. For some reason, my right turn blinker is on. Blink. Blink. Blink. In the rearview I can see what looks like bloody rags and pulp about twenty yards or so behind me, but my vision has been blurry of late. Blink. Blink. Blink. I see things in threes as I am off my pills and have been for awhile and will tell anyone concerned to go to hell about it.

Blink. Blink. Blink. Tommy moved out to California a couple of years back. He said he found work and then I said maybe he turned queer. He told me to go fuck myself. Who says that to their daddy? I ask you, gentle reader. But he moved off and didn't call anymore and I stopped getting my pills and now I hear Martha cooing to me from the kitchen and I see headlights out on the highway in threes. Threes for Christ sake. Blink. Blink. Blink. Martha in there doing the dishes. Putting cornbread in the oven. Humming a hymn. *Just As I Am* or *The Old Rugged Cross*. *Nearer My God To Thee*. I hear all that and sometimes get up out my easy chair with my peter in my hand and skulk into the kitchen to draw up behind her and lift that old skirt only to find that it's just me, alone, holding my limp shame.

That Claunch boy is a mess back there, but I wouldn't know which of the three piles I see to clean up. Blink. Blink. Blink. What a mess. What a damn mess. That radio preacher was trying to tell me something about bodies or my body or God's body or some horseshit. And before I squeal out and head for home, there comes a scream like some wildcat from back at the house. A scream cutting through my cracked window. Somebody screaming. A body screaming. Bodies is why I stopped going to church, why I closed up the station. Perfumed bodies. Talking gossiping singing bodies. Coughing, annoying, cloying, none-of-your-damn business busy bodies.

Poor little simple child. Wasn't meant to be, I reckon. Here I am in my seventh decade like some crusted-over boil upon this earth — ornery, insane, useless — while this ten-year-old gets blotted out on a Sunday afternoon. I stopped questioning the Almighty long ago, but Jesus, this one takes the damn cake. Nearer my god to thee.

Well, there's blood and bits of gristle all over the front of my car. Little bits of bone flecked up in the grill like bugs. Blood feathered out and spread across the hood and fender from me hauling ass home. Blood and gristle. Somebody screamed. Blink. Blink. Blink. I'll just sit here in this easy chair and wait for it. The Sheriff, if I'm lucky. Corn-drunk Joe, if I'm not.

Martha has gone quiet in the kitchen. Martha deep down in our plot beside her parents. Those unwanted little ones she had gone quiet out back behind the tool shed. Darling, I say. Honey, I say. This sure would be a fine time for one of your hymns. Just as I am, Martha. Just as I am.

Tires crunching the gravel out front. Daylight failing beyond the windows. I load a double-aught into the family shotgun and sit back and wait.

Pine Grove Blues

The driver is not young but looks it. Even with a white frosting on his chin wig and a paunch spreading above his lap, the face is soft and babyish; the dirty blonde hair tussled like a summertime lad's. He curses traffic around him, whipping the rental car to and fro like some video game spaceship. "Mongoloids!" he shouts, "Cretins! Lummoxes! Afterbirth!"

A woman is diminishing in the passenger seat, one hand clutching a Taco Bell bag, the other gripping the door handle. She possesses the strong facial features of some Biblical queen. Her skin the blue-black color of ripe eggplant. "Les, please slow down," she says, her eyes closing in anticipation of the bluster to come.

"Trying to make our check-in, darling!" he snarls. "I need a shower. You need a shower." He swerves into the right lane, horns honking. "This whole goddamn state needs a shower!"

An hour previous, they crawl along I-10 west of Baton Rouge, rain lashing off the bayou. Lester picks at his whiskers and says, "I think, if given the opportunity, your daddy would march me out into the darkest woods and put a bullet in my head." The car radio catches an old zydeco tune, accordion pumping, fiddles, shuffle beats.

The woman bites into her bean burrito and mumbles, "Oh Lester, you're such a flat-out racist."

Windshield wipers click in time with the zydeco for a couple of measures, then fall behind. "I didn't say he was going to pop a cap in my pasty-white ass!" Lester replies, his face shriveling like a dried up Christmas tangerine. "I know you're joking, Alice, but my god!"

He cranks the radio. More accordions and static. The song ends and a D.J. breaks in, speaking French. From what Lester can decipher, there's a crawfish festival the following weekend in Lake Charles. "The two things these folks excel at down here," Lester states, "music and food!" He glances at Alice. "And there you are, what with your corporate bean sludge." Lester's grease-stained bag of cracklings, purchased at that last pit stop outside of Hammond, is stinking up the car, but Alice holds her tongue.

Twenty-four hours previous, Lester is sitting by himself on a rotting picnic table south of Walnut, Mississippi. Throngs of folks nearby are gathered around a large fiery pit, smoke billowing up to mix with the late afternoon snow flurries. Alice is standing next to the pitmaster, her father, Bad Daddy McGee. She plays the dutiful, attentive prodigal daughter, visiting from the big city, laughing at his country-ass jokes and helping out to mop sauce on the goat meat. Bad Daddy owns a small chain of meat-and-three joints in the north Mississippi hill country, between Corinth and Olive Branch. He is a tiny man, all coiled and rippling with muscles. He left behind his granddaddy's and daddy's life of hard labor to become a shrewd small town businessman. On their family plot of land, he throws legendary goat barbecues several times a year, mostly for reunions and Christmas. Everyone is invited. There's fife and drum music and plenty to drink.

Lester hears the unmistakable call of a pileated woodpecker off in the pines. Just then, a thick-necked man in a *Fuck Tha Police* t-shirt approaches. He nods at Lester and grunts, "Medieval studies, huh?"

Lester's eyes widen, a snowflake landing on his pimply nose. "Yessir. I'm Alice's husband, Lester." He holds out his hand to Fuck Tha Police, who leaves him hanging.

"Mordor and shit, right?" The man swigs a Bud Light, tugging on his nuts. Lester glances over to see Alice giggling, holding the sauce mop out to swab down one of her sisters. She *seems* happy, he thinks. Those meds must be working. But by god, this is the last night here, and then we hit that old dusty trail.

"Well, not exactly," says Lester. The man cocks his head, waiting for more. "Um," he continues, "you see, Mordor doesn't exist. Never has."

Fuck Tha Police takes another swig and starts laughing. "Easy brah," he drawls, "just fucking wit' you." He lays a beefy hand upon Lester's shoulder. "King Arthur and Merlin and shit, right?"

Lester exhales a dry laugh. "Close enough," he says.

The Lafayette traffic is surprisingly heavy. All those transplants from Katrina, they've heard, have added to the city's population. Each red light on Pinhook Road cycles several times before they make it through an intersection. Lester drums on the steering wheel and cranes his head forward. "Goddamn but this looks like I-35 at rush hour."

Alice is staring out the passenger window at an old

raised Catholic cemetery. The rain has stopped for now and the streetlights cast a soft glow on the concrete tombs. Live oaks draped with Spanish moss stand like sentinels alongside the street. Her expression stays flat and she montones, "Almost there, sweetie."

Lester belches softly and turns up the radio volume. "Balfa Brothers," he says, a proud smirk appearing on his lips. "Man! What if our station back home played shit like this?"

Alice dismisses the question and cracks her window. She tilts her head towards it and closes her eyes and breathes in the desiccated air. It smells of molded leaves and wood smoke and standing pools of oily water reflecting the tired gray winter sky.

An older woman with a thick Cajun accent shows Lester and Alice around the bed and breakfast grounds after they've dropped their luggage off in the room. Courtyard lights shine on palmettos and banana plants and elephant ears thriving beneath the oaks and magnolias. Late December camellias and roses bloom by the back porch door. The house itself is a crumbling old antebellum, with touches of Spanish, and the gothic statuary and wrought iron tables and chairs in the courtyard give the garden just the barest hint of British formality. The night air is soft and warm, and Alice is visibly moved by the old world ambience of the place. The woman's name is Lucille, and Alice hangs on her every word, even laughing at the rote jokes. Lester, however, appears to be fighting off, and losing, a massive battle with heartburn, no doubt brought on by the fried pork skins. He rubs his upper belly vigorously, grimacing, glancing back towards their room in what was the servant's quarters. Finally, he apologizes and excuses himself.

Alice asks Lucille about the ghost. It was a feature on the place's website, and she and Lester had picked this place just for that reason. Something a little scary, maybe even diabolical, to liven up their routine. Lester, ever the grim agnostic, had laughed it off, but she got the sense that he really wanted to believe in it.

Lucille says, "Here's where it happened." They're standing in the parlor, all dark oak floors and crystal opulence. A tall sideboard holds various bottles of bourbon, rum, brandy. "The founder of this estate, Corporal Alfred Lambert, had just returned from his military duties abroad, up in Tennessee I believe, and some disgruntled landowner nearby snuck up on him and slit his throat from ear to ear. He was left to bleed out, right here where this rug lies. The man survived such carnage as Shiloh only to be slaughtered like a pig in his own parlor." Alice stares at the rug, a faded reddish Persian, and tries to imagine the young confederate sprawled there, gasping his last breaths. "Of course," Lucille continues, "one of the servants was blamed for it. They strung him up the very next day."

"My god," says Alice.

Lucille lowers her head, letting the gravitas of the moment, the historical atrociousness of it, linger. After a couple of well-rehearsed beats she says, "Yes. Those were ugly times, indeed." She then takes a step back and swings her left hand over to the sideboard. "Most of these decanters are later period acquirements for the Lambert family, but this one here belonged to Alfred himself." She runs her fingertips lightly along the cut crystal curves, the cognac inside glowing like a winter sunset. "Later this evening, you all can help yourself to a drink in here. And who knows, maybe the Corporal will join you."

They take late dinner at a dancehall called T-Don's just across the highway. Lester's belly is still fussy, and he nibbles at some French bread, dunking it in his smoked duck gumbo. Walking back to their room, Alice mentions the parlor, the ghost, the brandy beckoning. Reluctantly, Lester agrees for a tipple. No one's in the house, it seems, and this brightens his mood a bit.

"I'm sorry for what I said about Bad Daddy," he says after a sip. "You know that I admire and respect him. I mean — who wouldn't?" He sets down the tumbler, his left hand picking through his whiskers. "Are you OK?"

Alice can't tear her eyes away from the Persian rug. "I'm OK, Les," she whispers, "just a bit tired is all. I probably should turn in. You can stay up to toast the ghost if you want."

She gives his knee a pat, yawns, then leaves the parlor. Lester cuts a quick glance over to the decanters on the sideboard. Don't imagine old Lambert would mind me having another one, he thinks. After pouring a couple of fingers-worth, he lifts his tumbler and announces to the room in an overly dramatic drawl, "For the Sons of the South!"

The next morning dawns breezy and warm. Alice sits with her coffee in the courtyard; head back, listening to the soft piping of a wintering hermit thrush. An undisturbed edition of the day's *Lafayette Examiner* lies next to her elbow. Lester suddenly appears in a pink bathrobe, shuffling his flip-flops on the dew-slickened patio stones. He's clutching a prescription medication bottle, his face scrunched up like an old lady's. He shakes the bottle furiously to indicate the emptiness of it.

"How long have you been out?" he asks. A warm breeze lifts up his thinning bangs, his forehead shining in the bright bayou sun. "Aren't these daily?"

Alice's face is set in stone, her head still tilted back. "Are you snooping on me?" she hisses.

Lester guffaws. "I just know that these are really important for you," he says. "Forgive me for giving a shit." The thrush has moved in closer, piping softly from inside a thick cluster of banana plants. Alice sips at her coffee.

"Les," she say, "I've been off them for awhile. Never felt better . . . ."

"What? How long?"

"Listen. I feel like I really turned a corner here. I just don't need them anymore."

Lester steps in closer to the table, his flip-flopped feet set apart like a boxer, his bathrobe loosening in the breeze. "The reason you felt better is because the pills were *working*. That means you should keep taking them."

Alice sets her coffee down, leans her head back again and shuts her eyes. An eighteen wheeler honks from out on the highway. Wind rustling the banana fronds, the thrush piping. "I'm not going to talk about this right now," she whispers.

Lester shakes loose a couple of dry coughs. He cinches up his bathrobe, turns abruptly, and waddles back to the room.

After spending much of the day watching TV, Alice decides to dress up a bit and head to the parlor for an afternoon drink. Lester is out birdwatching. He had mentioned one of the local hot sauce plantations as being a hub for all sorts of marsh and water birds, neotropicals and such. Alice is able to breathe deeply and freely on these rare occasions that they are apart. Almost as if a hostage's pillowcase has slipped off her head.

Lucille is heading out the back door right when Alice steps in. "My, you look nice!" she says, beaming at Alice's little black dress and high heels ensemble. "Going out to dance later?"

"Yes, I think so," Alice replies. "Probably just back to T-Don's."

Lucille brushes past her and takes the steps down. "Ooh, yes. Tonight the Broussard Brothers play," she says. "I might see y'all there!"

Alice walks into the parlor and makes a beeline for the sideboard. She pours a healthy portion of brandy from the old confederate's decanter and then settles down in a plush velvet chair to study his portrait above the stone hearth. She suddenly thinks of that weird Jesus picture where his eyes follow the viewer around the room. Knocking back some cognac, Alice considers getting up and moving around the portrait. Instead, she laughs out loud and whispers, "I'm right here, old Lambert. Come spend some time with me . . . if you dare."

The room has darkened considerably when she wakes up. The last of the setting sun's rays peek through the nearest window and spotlight the empty tumbler on a table by her side. The glass glows a ghostly amber, as if still filled with brandy. Alice hears footsteps in the hallway, slow and shuffling.

"Any lifers today?" she calls.

The shuffling stops. Lester's windchapped face, pink

and shiny, pokes around the entryway into the parlor. He gives a weak grin and says, "A frigatebird . . . in flight."

"Wow. Really?" Alice sits up, alert now. "That's great, Les. Sorry I missed it."

Lester has been trying for a magnificent frigatebird for years. A tropical seabird, rare in the upper Gulf Coast, they do wander about, and their giant albatross-like wingspan makes them hard to miss in the sky. "That's OK," he says, "maybe next time. Oh, hey . . . have you heard the forecast? My god."

Heading toward the sideboard, he eyes the dwindling brandy, and glances over at Alice's empty tumbler and smirks. "Looks like I've got some catching up to do . . . ." He pours himself one and groans, knees popping, as he eases down on the couch. "You look fantastic, by the way."

Alice's face, which had softened from her nap and the small talk, now stiffens back into its mask, hard and statuesque. "I still do not want to talk about any of this," she says, her hands fidgeting and smoothing her dress at the knees over and over. "When we get home . . . I promise."

Lester sighs, his face hardening as well. "A tropical storm formed south of Houston a day or so ago and is heading our way overnight. They're talking tornados and hail. A foot of rain or more." He downs his drink in one big gulp and sighs again. "Aren't we below sea level here? Jesus . . . I'm thinking it might get ugly. What say we pack up and head out of town early?"

Alice laughs. She stands up, still smoothing out her dress, and says, "We'll be fine, Les. Our car's a rental, and covered. And we can just wait it out if the roads are flooded. They get this kind of stuff all the time around here. It'll be OK."

Their eyes lock for a moment. The first time in days, maybe weeks.

Lester's eyes cut away first. He hacks a dry cough and says, "Let me get cleaned up and we'll stroll over to T-Don's."

It's Friday night and the dancehall is packed. A portly old man on stage in blue jeans and denim work shirt and a cowboy hat methodically strums his acoustic guitar and sings French lyrics in a nasally whine. He leads his backing trio of fiddle, accordion, and drums — the Broussard Brothers — through all the Acadian classics. The music they make is rough-edged, yet ethereal. A crowd of locals waltz and swirl before them, and those just sitting and listening wear the faces of folks being raptured up to heaven.

Lester and Alice are seated at a back corner table, both picking at their dinners. Alice, still in some faraway fog, barely speaks to Lester, who is upset about Alice of course, but also agitated about the coming tropical storm. "How can these people laugh and drink and eat and dance at a time like this?" he snarls, glancing around the room at all the couples waltzing by.

Alice gives Lester a long quizzical look like he's some stranger in the street asking for directions to a place she's never heard of. She exhales sharply and excuses herself from the table for a restroom visit. "What?" snaps Lester, a bit louder and sharper than he had intended.

On the way out of the restroom a few minutes later, Alice spies an empty barstool next to a handsome young man in desert camouflage fatigues. Lester is still over at their table, his back to her, staring up at the corner television tuned to the Weather Channel. Alice can see, even from way back here, the monster storm churning up the Gulf of Mexico on the little TV radar. She heads for the bar.

"What are you having?" she asks the soldier. He glances up at her, a look of delight and surprise flashing across his lean clean-shaven face. "Rum and coke," he drawls, "Would you like one?"

Alice nods with a bright smile, her stomach suddenly fluttering like prom night. "I have time for a quick one," she says, slyly noting his hard physique beneath all that khaki. His cropped jet-black hair. His somewhat sad, far-seeing eyes. The young soldier smiles back and holds out his hand. "Name's Al. Al Lambert. Nice to meet you."

Lester realizes that he's been watching the tropical storm on a radar loop for quite some time now. T-Don's corner TV is all purple and red and yellow with its biblical horrors. "The sky was all purple, there were people running everywhere," Lester whispers aloud, and then giggles. His red beans and rice crusted-over and glutinous in its bowl. Alice's half po-boy sandwich lays untouched and limp atop a stack of greasy fries.

And suddenly he realizes that she's gone. He checks with the bartender, who responds with a Cajun shrug. She's gone. He knocks on the ladies' restroom door and calls out her name. Not here, someone shouts back from a stall. She's gone. She's off her meds for who knows how long, he thinks, and now she has walked out on me in south Louisiana right before a goddamn weather disaster.

Fat Gulf raindrops are pelting Lester as he darts across the highway. His heart is pounding. He's near to hyperventilating. "Fuck this," he yells. "Fuck this!"He bursts through their B & B door shouting "Alice!" like he did in T-Don's parking lot and back at the bar and outside the ladies' restroom. "Alice!" He had hoped that she was just fed up being around him and had come back to the room for some peace and quiet. "Alice!" No sign of her. She's gone. The sweetly scented mess of her dirty clothes spilling off the side of the bed. Her suitcase splayed open on the floor in the corner. She's gone. The TV left on. The volume down. The local radar looping such multicolored violence to come.

Mel Bay's Book of
the Dead

Young Ronald is investigating the give-away bins at his public library. Methodically, like an archaeologist brushing away layers of desert sand. Passing time waiting for his ride home from school, he flips through old issues of *Time* and *Life*, *AARP* newsletters, *Upper Room* devotionals and the like. His neighbor friend James squats by his side, also rummaging, and glancing every so often out the window to spy his mother's white Ford Futura coming down Pine Street. James snags an old *National Geographic* with a photo essay on some African tribe of bare-breasted women and bare-assed warriors. "Ronnie," he hiss-whispers in the voice of an explorer beholding Kilimanjaro for the first time, "look at them titties!" The word *titties* pops out louder than he means to, and the gray-headed librarian at the front desk shoots a frowning glance in their direction. James quickly rolls up the periodical and sticks it in his backpack for further observation at home.

James Hicks, just one year ahead of Ronnie in junior high, seems somehow even older, and owns a much-coveted G & L Les Paul-style guitar. He plays along with Skynyrd albums and the Stones, and he's actually pretty decent, Ronnie the bumbling beginner admits. Ronnie's dad enjoys using Spoonerisms, referring to the neighbor boy as "Hames Jicks," and he doesn't think too highly of James, or any of their other neighbors for that matter. When Ronnie asked for an electric guitar last Christmas, his dad muttered something about not being able to afford it. But deep down, Ronnie wondered if it was simply the fact that his dad might not want him turning out like a certain Hames Jicks.

As Mrs. Hicks pulls up into the library parking lot, Ronnie discovers an accordion file filled with sheet music, guitar magazines and tablature, back issues of *Rolling Stone* and *Cream*. Tucked deep inside the folder, he finds a blank drawing pad. It appears to be an ancient tablet of some sort. Yellowed and brittle. "Hey Ronnie," James shouts back through the closing glass door, "mom's here!" The tablet has light scratches and indentations on each page, but no sign of ink used anywhere. Strange, Ronnie thinks. Mysterious. Sniffing it, he realizes it gives off the slightest whiff of that China Palace buffet his church youth group visited recently. Where has this thing been? He ponders while stuffing it into his satchel.

A latchkey kid. That's what they call him. Ronnie's mother works evening shifts at the county hospital while his dad stays late most afternoons directing the Pinkard High School band. Both call him that lovingly, with more than a touch of pride. Our little latchkey kid. Even Mrs. Hicks says that while dropping him off from school. James, however, presses his face up against the passenger window as they pull away, sticking out his tongue and making fart noises.

The house is dark, cool, and quiet. Ronnie sets down his satchel and turns on the kitchen radio to that FM station his big sister told him about. A fuzz guitar suddenly blares from the tiny speaker, and then a lead vocalist belts out *American woman, stay away from me!* Why would he sing that? Ronnie thinks. Are American women to be avoided, or even feared? Are they dangerous or evil or something? He furrows his brow and pours some chocolate milk into an Alabama Crimson Tide cup. His mom doesn't seem evil, he thinks, though she does get fussy and angry quite often these days. He figures that it has something to do with her working odd hours. Mrs. Hicks is nice enough, what with giving him rides home from school and all. And his big sister is OK, and even kind of cool at times. Her boyfriend had recently loaned him a Silvertone guitar to practice on, along with a little Peavey amplifier.

Ronnie finishes his chocolate milk, turns off the radio, and slinks back to his room to snatch up the Silvertone. He remembers that strange old tablet in his satchel as he's emptying out his textbooks onto the bedroom floor: History, Biology, Geometry. He grabs the tablet and sets it on his bed, cuts on the amp and plugs in his guitar. Popping in his sister's 8-track tape of Foreigner's *Double Vision*, he starts struggling with the power chord intro for "Hot Blooded" and notices out of the corner of his eye that the tablet appears to be glowing. Throbbing even.

Saturday afternoon, and once again Ronnie has the house to himself — mother at work, dad judging a marching band contest. It's so quiet he feels as if his ears are going to pop. *Wind & Wuthering* by Genesis is cued up to go in his 8-track player. Laying back across his bed and closing his eyes, Ronnie lets the synthesizers and guitars and odd-timed drumbeats carry him away to some misty old English countryside, or even a craggy mountain peak with dwarves and elves preparing for battle. Those images fade as he drifts off into sleep.

A vast pasture stretches out before him. He's holding the tablet in his left hand and it pulses and glows. In his right, the Silvertone squeals feedback — a high harmonic G. And in the blue sky above him, a symbol appears: a looping snake-like maze figure. It hangs there, ancient and Chinese-looking, growing brighter and brighter. The feedback squeal grows as well, louder and louder, before morphing into heavenly bell sounds. Ronnie wakes and bolts up out of bed. It's Hames Jicks calling from next-door, letting the phone ring and ring.

Hank Jr. is drawling and whooping it up from the Hicks family turntable. James' parents are out getting groceries at the Jitney Jungle, so the two boys are alone before a cranked stereo with both their guitars plugged-in and amplifiers turned up. "*A country boy can survive . . .*" James snarl-sings while pick-scraping his Les Paul copy.

Ronnie is still a tad groggy from his nap. And that bizarre symbol he saw hanging in the dream's blue sky still flashes in his mind. It reminds him of when he stares long enough at the preacher up in his Sunday morning pulpit, and then, by closing his eyes he can see the preacher's image like some bright white aura outlined by darkness.

"*And if you ain't into that we don't give a damn!*" James shouts out along with Hank. He has his legs spread wide and he windmills his right arm across the G & L like Pete Townshend. The songs ends, but Ronnie is still giggling even as James picks the 45 up off the turntable and gingerly puts it back in its sleeve. "Hey James," Ronnie hiccups, "put on some Foreigner." And before long, the live version of "Hot Blooded" is blasting through the Hicks' household.

Both boys are chunking away on the overdriven power chords and grunting and nodding their shaggy heads like Paleolithic man. James gets all rared up to take the midsection solo like he usually does, but it's Ronnie all of sudden, amped-up and blasting out the opening riff. His fingers have taken over. What the hell? He thinks. Smooth legato bends giving way to lightning-fast blues licks. Hammer-ons and pull-offs.

Ronnie stares down at his furious fingers like he's witnessing some black magic ritual. James steps back, both hands dropped to his side. His eyes open wide, his face pale. His guitar humming like an AM radio tuned to static.

As the weeks pass by and his school year draws to a close, Ronnie becomes aware of quieter rides home from Mrs. Hicks, and from James especially. Fewer and fewer afternoon phone calls, and then none. That Saturday at the Hicks home in which Ronnie cut loose on a maniacally inspired and otherworldly guitar solo seems to have created a rift between the two of them. James avoids Ronnie in the hallways, and now sits with older marching band boys at their lunch table. Ronnie feels hurt of course, and a bit angry at times, but he now totes around his Silvertone and amp between classes, a perpetual show-and-tell, and even has a small fan club of sorts. Strange and underdeveloped little creatures from choir class gather around him, like pimply disciples bearing gifts of soggy corn dogs and Fritos. *Can you play this song, Ronnie?* Mumbles, then a Chuck Berry riff, or Jimi. *Can you play that song, Ronnie?* More mumbles, then some Sabbath. But he barely notices them, his fanclub. His tablet lays open beside an untouched lunch. Symbols flashing that, apparently, only he can see. The very binding itself throbbing and humming.

And no one is more surprised by his newfound shredding abilities than Ronnie himself, and over the course of his matriculating years in Pinkard he only gets better. Less and less time spent on homework, more and more time in front of the stereo while cradling his Silvertone. He had even appeared on stage with a Top 40 cover band playing senior prom last month, word about him having gotten around. He was asked to step up and rip high-octane solos on Huey Lewis, The Cars, even some Steely Dan. The pats on his back from the other musicians and the applause from older classmates made him feel — as best as he could tell — "high." High like those rednecks say they get smoking their funny cigarettes beneath the bleachers cutting class. High like Hames Jicks said he felt after once swallowing a cup of his uncle's Mason jar hooch.

All this time, month after month, Ronnie had been flipping through the blank tablet as he practiced his chords and scales, his riffs and licks. Strange symbols still appearing on the pages, wavy, dreamlike. But of late, the thing simply stays put and unopened on his bedside table, softly glowing, a nightlight of sorts. No need for him to study it anymore during lunch, or gaze at it while hunched over in the bleachers for gym class. His chops are miraculously at the level of a seasoned touring musician. A lifer. A genuine rock and roll guitar hero. And those mystical drawings now appear before him simply when he closes his eyes, either sleeping or just zoning out. Back row of American history? English literature? There they are, floating, shimmering, pulsating . . . .

The summer before his senior year, Ronnie shelves books and works the circulation desk at the public library. He upgrades to a small Marshall amplifier to go along with the used black Telecaster his parents got him for Christmas. He forms his own cover band, and they book Saturday afternoon gigs at the city park swimming pool pavilion. Nothing fancy. Early Stones and Beatles, Creedence. Mostly it's the kid's parents who stand around watching, listening, bobbing their heads and smiling and clapping. These guys are *really* good, they whisper, maybe a little too good for their age, don't you think? The kids themselves, all younger classmates (the older ones hanging out down at the river, drinking and smoking), are too busy belly flopping and playing Marco Polo to notice.

After James Hicks graduates Pinkard High, a night clerk position opens up at the *Dixie Flicks* video store. He applies, interviews, and lands it. Welding school can wait, he explains to his parents. They reluctantly agree after he tells them he will stay at home, behave, and save up his earnings for trade school tuition down the road. What he doesn't tell them is that a gold-top Les Paul sits packed-up on layaway with his name on it at a guitar shop over in Decatur. Or that he will spend five nights a week on his ass sneak drinking and hidden behind a store counter watching low-budget slasher movies, soft-core European films, *Faces of Death*, and worse.

By late September, James has saved enough to bring home his new guitar. With just too much pride for him to contain, he decides to rub it in with his old neighbor friend. He catches Ronnie's mom one afternoon on her way out the door and asks if Ronnie is around.

"Why sure, hon," she replies, her eyebrows raised slightly in surprise. "We haven't seen hide nor hair of you in ages, boy. Where you been?"

"Uh. Video store mostly." James stares up and over her and down the hallway towards Ronnie's room. "I work there full-time now."

"Well...you just go on back, hon. He's in his room playing that guitar."

The awkward silence in Ronnie's bedroom doesn't last long, as James clicks open his road-case and pulls out the Les Paul, still shiny from the shop. "Check this shit out," he practically smirks. Ronnie sits blushing upon his bed, embarrassed on behalf of Hames Jicks and his pathetic need to show-off, embarrassed for all the time that has passed since they've last spoken, embarrassed for the unnecessary loss of their friendship.

"Wow, James," he deadpans, "Looks awesome." From other side of the house, the kitchen phone rings.

"Aw hell, man, you should hear it wail!" James plucks the intro hook to ZZ Top's *LaGrange* as Ronnie brushes past him to answer the phone. It's Ronnie's dad, staying late again for snare, tom, and percussion sectional rehearsals. "These *dummers* always need extra practice time, Ron. Always."

"I hear you, dad."

"Is your mother still there?"

Down the hall, James is sitting on Ronnie's bed, still absent-mindedly noodling the ZZ Top riff and sniffing about the room. His gaze lands on the old tablet lying on a bedside table, and James seems to recall, years ago, Ronnie mentioning the weird visions he had beheld within this thing's pages. And dreamt even. How the symbols floated about whenever he closed his eyes to daydream, or to sleep. How they quivered and hummed. How his fingers likewise quivered and twitched right up until the moment he would attach them to a six-string axe plugged into an amplifier. Then they would flutter and fly with a mind of their own. All of this he had confided in James on that very afternoon of his first guitar freak-out at the Hicks' home. Afterwards, James had bashfully asked to borrow it, but Ronnie said he wouldn't be able to. He said that he had to keep the thing close by him at all times. A "talisman" was the word he had used. He said that originally, he thought that it was his own self finding the tablet, but that eventually he came to realize — the *tablet found him* instead.

James cuts his eyes towards the open bedroom door. He blinks once, then twice. Inhales, exhales. He can hear Ronnie still talking on the phone, laughing. And in one quick sweeping motion, he rises from the bed while snatching up the tablet. He drops it into his guitar case, and quickly places his Les Paul on top of it. Rushing down the hall, James punches Ronnie hard on his shoulder while simultaneously belching, "Later."

The tablet is gone. Ronnie intuits it. He feels it before he's even able to see with his own eyes and register it for a fact. James took it, he thinks. He knows. He feels it. Why would James take it, he wonders. Because I can play guitar like Brian May or Mark Knopfler, or anybody else that I hear, and he's just still farting around on Jimmy Buffet songs like a church youth group leader. That's why, he thinks. That's why, he knows.

He is in the vast pasture again. Blue sky. No wind. Above him, all the tablet symbols he has ever beheld over the years have amassed, and all are hovering and humming. His dream-self stands below, dumb, miniscule. The hum now coalescing around a low register G major chord. The people's key, he heard someone say once. A low G, warmly distorted and wavering slightly like from analog tape. Like his sister's 8-track cassettes sound after they've sat in the backseat of her yellow Pinto on a blistering summer afternoon outside the city pool. Like that, only much louder, much more magnificent and menacing . . . .

The kitchen phone is ringing again. Ronnie can hear his dad snoring like a freight train from his parent's bedroom, so he gets up, still shaky and murky from the dream, still hearing that immense distorted G chord, and he stumbles down the hall to answer it.

"Hon, I'm sorry to wake you."

His mom's voice inside the telephone speaker at this late hour. Early hour? She's still at the county hospital working her shift. He can hear phone beeps and voices murmuring in the background. A deep man's voice yelling something. More beeps.

"Hon, are you there?"

"Mom. Yeah. What's up?"

"Listen, babe, I want you to sit down now." A pause. "There's been a terrible accident. A car wreck." Another pause. More phone beeps. More murmuring background voices. "It's James, hon . . . ."

Ronnie sits at the kitchen table and stares down at the floral print Dollar Store placemats with coffee rings. He picks at some toast crumbs as his mom describes the carnage EMS just cleaned up out on River Road, at that dark woodsy curve right before it joins up with the highway. The Hicks family's old Ford Futura, the one James had been using since his junior year, had run off the edge of the road, down a slope, ending up flipped-over and wrapped around a one hundred-year-old white oak. The car had caught fire, torching the tree trunk and the sage grass all around, and pretty much melted and burned everything inside and outside down to a fine char. No other automobiles were involved, or even anywhere nearby when it happened. The cause of it all unknown.

"I'm so sorry, hon . . . I don't know what to say."

Ronnie closes his sleep-puffy eyes, trying to absorb the shock while awaiting some sort of onslaught of grief. He pictures James and his Les Paul, just hours ago, goofing off down the hall in his room. He thinks of how angry he was, again just hours ago, for realizing that the tablet was gone and that James had taken it. He keeps his eyes closed, and can see James upside-down in the crushed Ford, his new guitar and the tablet he'd just stolen stowed away in the trunk, all going up in a blaze. Ronnie waits for tears to come. He keeps his eyes shut tight and simply waits for the tears.

"Hon, are you still there? Are you OK?"

"Yeah."

As his mom continues talking, Ronnie notices that the symbols are gone. His eyes have been shut for over a minute now, and those mysterious shapes aren't there. No quivering ancient symbols. No low distorted humming. Just blackness. Just nothing.

"Listen babe," his mom says, "don't wake up your dad . . ."

No tears yet. Ronnie opens his eyes. The coffee rings

are still in their same place. The toast crumbs. No tears. His mom is talking, saying something about his dad and school tomorrow, but he's not listening anymore because the symbols are gone. Still no tears. He flicks his fingers and notices that they're numb. Not quivering, not twitching. Just numb. He sets the phone down on the table, his mom's voice tiny, crumb-sized, and he floats dreamily down the hall to his bedroom.

Ronnie stares at his Telecaster. It's leaning back against his bedside table, half-hidden in the shadows like an old friend who he's fallen out with. He picks it up. The symbols are gone, the humming is gone, his fingers are numb. He picks up the guitar and simply holds it. He is scared shitless, and not sure of just what to do next.

Acknowledgements

Thanks be to Ashley Savage Williams, Scott Alexander Jones, David Melanson, and Elizabeth Rogers for their loving support and assistance with these stories. A wholehearted thank you goes out to William Pate and Ash Lange for their excitement over this ragtag collection, and their hard work in making it into an actual book.

Destination Dollywood story idea stolen from Allen Michie.

Dwayne from Texas story title stolen from Robert Harrison.

About the Author

Harold Whit Williams is a prize-winning poet and longtime guitarist for the indie rock band Cotton Mather. He is the recipient of the 2020 FutureCycle Poetry Book Prize, the *Mississippi Review* Poetry Prize, and the Robert Phillips Poetry Chapbook Prize. The author of five books of poetry, Williams lives in Austin, Texas where he records lo-fi music as Daily Worker and catalogs the KUT Collection for the University of Texas Libraries. *Mel Bay's Book of the Dead* is his first book of short stories.

Other Works by Harold Whit Williams

Poetry:

- *My Heavens*
- *Red Clay Journal*
- *Lost in the Telling*
- *Backmasking*
- *Waiting For The Fire To Go Out*

About the Publisher

SAR Press
Austin

Mel Bay's Book of the Dead is the first non-journal book-length publication of *San Antonio Review*'s new book publishing imprint, *San Antonio Review* Press.

SAR Press, an imprint of *San Antonio Review*, Texas' international literary, arts and ideas journal since 2017, is devoted to publishing book-length works by interesting voices. SAR Press is composed of *San Antonio Review* Editorial Collective members William O. Pate II in Austin and Ash Lange in Cumbernauld, Scotland.

San Antonio Review is Texas' international literary, arts and ideas journal. Founded in 2017 in San Antonio and based in Austin, *SAR* serves as a space outside academia, traditional media, corporations and government for scholars, activists, parents, students, artists, writers and others interested in sharing to build a better collective community.

San Antonio Review publishes original essays, poetry, art, reviews, theory and other work twice a week on its website. Print issues are published twice a year in June and November. Founded in 2017 in San Antonio and based in Austin, SAR is devoted to serving as a gathering space outside academia, the market and government for writers, artists, scholars, activists, workers, students, parents and others to express their perspectives and reflections on our shared world and help develop visions of our collective future. Funded by its publisher's income from his day jobs, donations and the sale of print editions and other materials and led and maintained by an all-volunteer editorial collective, SAR is not beholden to any institution, organization or ideology. As an open-access journal, SAR is available free online.

Manuscript submissions should be directed to:

San Antonio Review
ATTN: Press Submissions
SAN ANTONIO REVIEW
2028 E BEN WHITE BLVD #240-5735
AUSTIN TX 78741

For more on *San Antonio Review*, visit sareview.org. For direct-from-publisher purchasing, visit 787atx.me.